Cast

John J. Malone. A short, plump
whiskey and keeping blondes fro...

Jake Justus. A redheaded press agent, manager, ex-reporter and sometime amateur detective.

Helene Brand. Blonde, beautiful and rich, she can out drink and out drive most men. She's in love with Jake but has trouble getting him to the altar.

Nelle Brown. She's the singing star of a popular radio program. She married for money but fell in love with her husband.

Henry Gibson Gifford or "Tootz". Nelle's much older husband, a former millionaire socialite who lost his money and most of his marbles shortly after marrying Nelle. He sees horses in the living room and says men are following him.

Macy McKee or "Baby." He's the latest of Nelle's young lovers. He'd do anything for her but he knows her heart belongs to Tootz.

Paul March. He used to be Nelle's lover. Now he's a corpse who won't stay put.

Daniel Von Flanagan. He added the "Von" so people wouldn't think he was just another Irish cop. He'd rather raise minks that catch crooks.

Molly Coppins. Paul March's helpful landlady.

Willie Wolff. Paul March's neighbor. He likes his beer.

John St. John. An ad executive, he's a shifty type with a Boston accent and a Nebraska pedigree.

Essie St. John. His frequently unfaithful wife. No one blames her. She's no beauty but doesn't have trouble finding men who appreciate her.

Bob Bruce. Nelle's big, blond and handsome announcer.

Lou Silver. Nelle's director, he chases women but seldom catches one.

Oscar Jepps. Nelle's producer, he's fat, gentle and kindhearted.

Joe McIvers. He's an ad man who appears never to sleep.

Schultz. Nelle's control engineer.

Papa Goldman. Nelle's sponsor, he made a fortune selling candy.

Mr. Givvus. Back in Philadelphia he made his fortune in soap, now he'd like to sponsor Nelle's program.

The John J. Malone books
8 Faces at 3 (1939)
The Corpse Steps Out (1940)
The Wrong Murder (1940)
The Right Murder (1941)
Trial by Fury (1941)
The Bid Midget Murders (1942)
Having Wonderful Crime (1943)
The Lucky Stiff (1945)
The Fourth Postman (1948)
Knocked for a Loop (1957)
My Kingdom for a Hearse (1957)
But the Doctor Died (1967)
(It is highly unlikely that this was actually
written by Rice)
The Pickled Poodles (1960)
(an authorized continuation of the Malone series
by Larry Harris, aka Laurence M. Janifer)

Short story collections
The Name is Malone (1958)
People Vs. Withers and Malone (1963)
(with Stuart Palmer, who maintained Rice
participated in the plotting of
the stories)
Once Upon a Train
(with Stuart Palmer, edited by
Harold Straubing)
Murder, Mystery & Malone (2002)
edited by Jeffrey Marks

The standalone novel
Home Sweet Homicide (1944)
has been reprinted by
The Rue Morgue Press

The Corpse Steps Out

A John J. Malone mystery by

Craig Rice

Rue Morgue Press

Lyons, Colorado

About Craig Rice

"Murder is not mirthful and there is nothing comic about a corpse," Craig Rice wrote in a 1946 essay, "Murder Makes Merry," for Howard Haycraft's *The Art of the Mystery Story*. Yet Rice herself was able to make murder mirthful, perhaps because she made it abundantly clear that it was all in good fun. "She never forgot," said critic J. Randolph Cox, "that the primary purpose of the detective story was entertainment."

And entertain readers she did. She got serious once in a while, in the novels written as by Michael Venning or in the stand-alone, *Telefair*, but for the most part she went for the laugh, especially in a dozen or so novels featuring Chicago criminal lawyer John J. Malone and his sidekicks, Jake and Helene Justus. Starting in 1939 with *8 Faces at 3* and ending with *My Kingdom for a Hearse* in 1957, published two weeks after her death at the age of 49, Rice's inebriated trio of sleuths prowled the streets and bars of Chicago, vowing that no blonde—or redhead or brunette—would ever be convicted of murder. Mostly, they hung out in Joe the Angel's City Hall Bar where they playfully tweaked the nose of homicide cop Daniel von Flanagan (he added the "von" so as not to be deemed just another Irish cop). Such antics eventually earned her the unheard of sum (for a mystery writer) of $46,000 a year by 1945 and in 1946 *Time* put her on its cover, the only mystery writer ever to be so honored.

While her nonseries book, *Home Sweet Homicide* (1944), in which the three children of a mystery writing single mom attempt to solve a murder and at the same time find their mother a man, won her much praise and a place in the Haycraft-Queen Cornerstone list, it is the Malone books that she is best known for. Yet, when the books first came out readers weren't all together sure who to call the primary sleuth among our hard-drinking, hard-living trio. In fact, the first paperback edition of *8 Faces at 3* proclaims it a "Jake Justus mystery."

However, while Jake and Helene get most of the ink, it's Malone who actually does the leg work (when he wasn't eye-balling some blonde's actual legs) and figures out whodunit. As series progresses, Malone increasingly occupies center stage. But Jake is the one who gets the girl when Helene eventually marries him.

While Jake and Malone are old pals, Helene enters their life for the first time in *8 Faces at 3* when she rushes into the room of the murdered woman's house like a "small cyclone." She's an admitted Northshore deb but she soon proves she can trade wisecracks with the best of them and drink both Malone and Jake under the table. Booze was a big part of their lives, as it was with their creator, and there's little doubt that it played a major role in Rice's death at age 49.

Jake explains that booze helps him think. Malone doesn't offer any explanations. But there's no doubt that this permanently disheveled lawyer knows his stuff. When the cops arrest Holly Inglehart for the murder of her aunt, Jake proclaims that there's no better lawyer in Chicago to represent her than Malone, explaining that he's "a lawyer who could get her out of trouble if she'd committed a mass murder in an orphanage, with seventeen policemen for witnesses." Malone preferred his clients be innocent but as long as they paid, he was willing to do everything in his considerable powers to help them beat the rap. It wasn't that he liked criminals, he just disliked society more. And as soon as he proved his client innocent and showed the cops how someone else did it he would immediately offers his services to the newly accused. The idea of someone going to the chair appalled him.

Rice's comic touch was ideally suited to her era. When FDR took office in 1933, he promised the country that happy days were here again. After more than three years of the Great Depression, people were ready for a belly laugh. They wouldn't have to wait long. In 1934, the era of the screwball comedy was ushered in by one unforgettable movie and an equally memorable mystery novel.

The movie was Frank Capra's *It Happened One Night*. This madcap comedy about a spoiled little runaway rich girl and a hard-bitten reporter was warmly embraced by the movie-going public and earned an unprecedented five major Oscars. The book was Dashiell Hammett's last novel, *The Thin Man.* "The generation of the Thirsty Thirties fell on it with huzzahs. It was a book they understood, regardless of being a mystery," wrote Lee Wright, Craig Rice's editor at Simon & Schuster. Critic and mystery writer William L. DeAndrea agreed. "It... established what has been called the zany, gin-soaked school of hardboiled mystery, where most of the violent events are played for laughs." Ironically, Hammett never published another novel, although he did not die until 1961, and most critics dismissed *The Thin Man* because it was atypical of his other work and was the basis for a series of commercially successful movies as well as a radio series.

But others followed in his footsteps. While directors such as Capra and Preston Sturges turned the screwball comedy into a movie art form, several mystery writers aped Hammett's style in print. His first major disciple was Jonathan Latimer, who published five novels, starting in 1935 with *Murder in the Madhouse*, featuring Bill Crane, a young, handsome, wise-cracking private eye who was equally at home swilling gin with lowlifes or sipping martinis in high society. Alcohol was the fuel, according to DeAndrea, that fed the detective muse in Latimer's books. It was also a key element in many other zany mysteries of the day, including Elizabeth Dean's 1938 *Murder is a Collector's Item*, which features a trio of sleuths with many similarities to Rice's characters, although Dean pushed her female character—an antiques store clerk—into the central role and relegated her wannabe private-eye boyfriend to escort duties. The booze continued to flow in Elliot Paul's 1939 debut, *The Mysterious Mickey Finn*, and Pam and Jerry North were at least as fond of their martinis as their cats in Frances and Richard Lockridge's sophisticated comedy-mysteries beginning with *The Norths Meet Murder* in 1940. If Doan, the private-eye antihero of Norbert Davis' 1943 *The Mouse in the Mountain* (and two other novels), is ever hesitant to take a drink, it's only because he fears his sidekick, an enormous Great Dane named Carstairs, would rip his throat out if he did.

Humor, if not booze, also found its way into the traditional cozy mystery of the early to mid-1930s. There had always been elements of humor in books by Ellery Queen, Rex Stout, and John Dickson Carr, but nothing like the out-and-out farce to be found in the works of Charlotte Murray Russell, in which an overbearing "full-figured" spinster sleuth browbeats the local police into letting her lend a hand in solving murders. Humor also was the dominant factor in the homespun mysteries of Phoebe Atwood Taylor featuring Asey Mayo, the "Codfish Sherlock." Among the wackiest mysteries of the period were the first of 21 books by two Australian-born sisters, Constance & Gwenyth Little, who launched their careers with the 1938 shipboard murder comedy, *The Grey Mist Murders*. The lighthearted Hildegarde Withers mysteries of Stuart Palmer featured an elderly school teacher and her (sort of) cop boyfriend, characters who were as popular with readers as they were with moviegoers. Several of Rice's own books were filmed, including *Home Sweet Homicide* and a couple of the Malones. Pat O'Brien, who resembled the Malone of the books, was one of the actors who portrayed him on the screen.

Many people think Craig Rice is a pseudonym but it was her legal name She was born in 1908 to Bosco Craig, a would-be painter, and his wife, Mary, a would-be sculptress, who named the little girl Georgiana. Bosco was in Europe when his daughter was born and Mary soon joined him, leaving her baby behind with Craig's mother. Living in the same house were Craig's half-sister, Nan Rice, and her husband Elton, who, though in their forties, gladly agreed to raise the young girl, not being able to conceive a child themselves. The Craigs retrieved their daughter once for a period of three years before again heading for Europe and handing her off to the Rices. When Georgiana was eleven, Mary Craig attempted to take her back once more, only to have her daughter tell her to "go to hell." The Rices formally adopted her and she became Georgiana Craig Rice. Eventually she dropped the Georgiana but not the attitude.

Toward the end of her career, the woman who had ghosted the occasional celebrity mystery (the Gypsy Rose Lee mysteries were not among them as most authorities now believe that Gypsy, a friend of Craig's, actual wrote her own books) had to rely on ghost writers herself in order to meet a deadline. When Rice wrote her editor, Lee Wright, and asked if she had read her latest manuscript yet, Wright famously responded: "Yes, have you?" She lived her life to excess and died way too young. And if the laughter had left her life at the end, it lives on in her books.

Tom and Enid Schantz
Lyons, Colorado

CHAPTER 1

Everything in the big, shabby room was painfully familiar. Not one thing had been changed in the months since she had seen it last. There were the same faded tan curtains at the window, one still hanging a little askew; the same pictures; even the same discolored spot on the wall over the fireplace.

She stood for one moment, listening. Nothing stirred. Yet for that moment she had found herself waiting for someone to speak.

It was a room she had never thought to see again. Certainly not on such an errand. Suddenly she shuddered, one hand grasping a sharp corner of the mantel for support, remembering the last time she had seen it, when she had walked out swearing it was the last time.

Involuntarily her eyes turned toward the floor of the kitchenette. The light from a tarnished bridge lamp reflected on the little pool of blood that seemed like a shadow reaching out toward the room. Once more she resisted an impulse to turn and flee.

Was someone watching her?

No, that was impossible. She had shut and locked the door. There was no one, could be no one, save herself, alive in the room.

Yet everywhere she turned, she could feel eyes following.

Suddenly she noticed that the tips of four pale fingers showed beneath the dingy green curtains of the kitchenette. For an instant, she clung to the mantel, fighting back the waves of weakness and nausea that threatened to engulf her. What if she should faint, here in this room, alone with that thing in the kitchenette? What if someone should come in and find her here?

For the barest breath of time, she decided in favor of flight.

But she knew there could be no escape from the thing she still had to do. It was the voice coming from the radio set that reminded her. Suddenly she was aware that it was still going on. All this time the radio had been going, dance music, voices, crazy rhythms, singing, laughter.

Had it been turned on, she wondered, an hour before?

She detached her fingers slowly from the edge of the mantel and walked over to the window, telling herself that right now in ten thousand, a hundred thousand, a million rooms, loud-speakers were still turned on, families still gathered before their radio sets. Not so very long ago switches had clicked and listeners had settled back in their easy chairs to wait for *her* voice. Right now, out on the Pacific coast, more listeners were eying their clocks, making ready to tune in on the rebroadcast.

Now, between broadcasts, there was the thing she must do.

One long indrawn breath, her eyes closed, and then she walked slowly around the room, carefully avoiding the soiled green curtains of the kitchenette, reassuring herself with the touch of familiar objects, the look of familiar things.

Suddenly a voice, deep, warm, chocolatish, came from the loudspeaker.

"You're nobody's sweetheart now. . . ."

She wheeled to stare at the object of wood and wire, and, as she turned, a grotesque flicker of light momentarily transformed the finger tips below the kitchenette curtains into living, curling, and then uncurling things.

"It just don't seem right, somehow,

That you're nobody's sweetheart now. . . ."

With one quick frenzied movement, she clicked the singing thing off in the middle of a word.

In the unsuspected silence, the harsh, indisputable ticking of a clock reminded her that she had very little time left. At the sound of it, her strength seemed to return. All at once she ceased to be the great radio star, the photographed and glamorous personality, the wife of a well-known socialite, the protected darling of the fan magazines. She was back in her childhood again, back in the days when every mouthful of food depended on resource and cunning, when each day's living had to be fought for with desperation. She could still fight, she reminded herself, with the same cunning, the same desperate frenzy.

Resolutely she wrenched her eyes away from the kitchenette and began searching the room, hurriedly, frantically, but still with a sort of disordered efficiency. No one in the world—no one alive in the world—knew that room better. She searched the imitation spinet desk, with the long cigarette burn still showing on the veneer, remembering with a little shudder the night it had been made there. Nothing in the desk but newspaper clippings and unpaid bills. The chest of drawers in the closet was only a confusion of soiled shirts and socks. She hunted through the book-shelves, filled with inexpensive and unread editions of standard classics, and pulled out one book after another, shaking it, reaching behind the rows. She felt under the pillows of the double bed that disguised itself as a studio couch, extended experimental fingers under the mattress.

There was still the little hiding place behind the cheap Venetian mirror, where they had once left notes for each other. She lifted out the mirror, ran her fingers carefully along the ledge, while purplish dust accumulated on her finger tips. Nothing there. Nothing but one discarded hairpin, dust-covered and rusted. She held it a moment on the palm of her hand, staring at it, and recognizing it as her own. Had it been there all this time?

But the thing she had come to find, the thing she must find, the reason for her terrible errand, was nowhere in the shabby room.

Was she being watched?

She stood, breathless, listening. There was the faint dripping of water from the cold-water faucet in the kitchenette. (Hadn't that faucet been fixed in all these months?) It sounded like the slow, remorseless, inexorable ticking of a clock.

There was so little time left!

Again she held herself back from headlong flight. Too much depended on her now. So much? Everything! Surely, she told herself, it was not so terrible a thing to do. Worse things had been done in this world, and bravely, too. Yes, even she herself had done them.

She was not only fighting for herself. There were others to fight for, she remembered them one by one, while slowly the courage she had lost came back to her.

There was no other way.

She went into the kitchenette, knelt on the floor, and carefully, methodically, began searching the dead man's pockets.

CHAPTER 2

The tall thin man in the little control room of the broadcasting studio stretched his long legs uncomfortably under the black-and-chromium table, absent-mindedly mussed up his red hair with a carelessly straying hand, and tried to focus his tired mind on the implications of what had just been said to him.

The forty-seventh broadcast of the Nelle Brown Revue had ended in a burst of applause from the studio audience. He forced his thoughts back over past events: Schultz, the control engineer, had made a final twisting of dials and switches, grabbed his hat, and gone hurrying off to get a sandwich between shows. Joe McIvers, from the advertising agency, had popped out of the booth like a cork out of a bottle to phone the sponsor. The usual procession of actors, musicians, sound men, and assistants had filed out of the studio.

Then Nelle Brown had blown into the little glass booth like a small tornado, her face dead-white against her deep-rose dress, her eyes smoking with fury. She had kicked the door shut, cursed the apparatus that kept it from slamming, and said, "Jake, I'm being blackmailed."

There had been a pause while he stared at her, before she lit a cigarette, took one long puff, stamped it out below the NO SMOKING sign, added, "I'm damned if I will!" and vanished.

The import of what she had been saying began to take form in his mind. Suddenly he sprang to his feet. Part of the duty of a press-agent manager, he told himself, was to keep one's client from being blackmailed.

What the devil had happened to Nelle Brown this time?

There was no sign of her in the corridor. He stopped a page boy.

"Miss Brown, sir? Try the reception room."

She was not in the reception room.

"Nelle? I saw her beat it down the elevator."

He caught the next elevator. It was crowded and stopped at every floor like an old-fashioned milk train. Nelle was nowhere in the lobby, nor in the bar nor the restaurant nor the cigar stand.

Jake Justus, press agent, manager, and ex-reporter, wondered again why, with untold billions of people in the world, everything had to pick him to happen to.

He lit a cigarette and tried to think. Nelle hardly ever left the studios between broadcasts. Could she possibly have gone home? But why the hell should she do that?

He might try it anyway, if he could manage without alarming Tootz, in case she hadn't gone home.

He stepped in the cigar stand, called Nelle's apartment. No one answered. He stood holding the receiver a long time, finally put it down, and methodically called every place Nelle might have gone.

After half a dozen calls, it was apparent that she had vanished into the very thinnest of air.

Damn it! he had to find her. He looked at his watch and frowned at its reminder of only forty minutes left until the rebroadcast for the West Coast.

Just at that moment, the idea came.

It was almost impossible. No, by God, it wasn't at all impossible. That was the one person most likely to be blackmailing Nelle. Why the devil hadn't he thought of it before, instead of wasting all this time? He ran out to the curb, hailed a taxi, gave the driver an address on Erie Street, and told him for Pete's sake to make it snappy.

The taxi stopped before a long, dark building. Jake told the driver to wait, bounded up the steps into a many-cornered hall, and climbed the unlighted stairs to the second floor. The air resounded with riotous tumult from one of the apartments, a very devil of a row. He grinned. He'd gone to a few parties in that building himself! For a moment he wished he didn't have the rebroadcast to attend. Not that he knew the people giving the party, but that would make no difference. Then he remembered his errand, and stopped grinning.

He knocked at a door marked 215 and waited. There was no answer. He noted a light shining through the transom and knocked again, louder. Hard to hear anything, with that infernal racket going on. He gave one last, violent pound and the door, slightly ajar, fell open.

Nelle was not there. No one was in the room.

He went in slowly and cautiously, wondering what to do next. Then he saw it in the kitchenette, crumpled on the floor—the man Nelle Brown might have come to see, the man who might have been blackmailing her— a dark huddle on the linoleum, in a little pool of blood.

The man was dead. Shot, Jake thought grimly, and not half shot. Nothing could be done for him now.

He stood there a moment, one hand twisting the shabby green curtains of the kitchenette. The thought of calling the police rose to his mind and was instantly dismissed.

Blackmail or no blackmail, why had she done it?

He reminded himself this was no time to spend thinking it over. Nelle might have left some trace of herself. Moving quickly and carefully, he looked through the room. There was nothing.

At last he went cautiously through the dead man's pockets, found no souvenir nor reminder of Nelle Brown. There was a surprisingly fat packet of twenty-dollar bills in the dog-eared wallet, and Jake scowled. Where the devil had all that money come from? The man had been broke, hungry broke, a week ago. Now, here was a fistful of folding money. Jake felt a pang of sympathetic regret. For all the man had been a rat, it was a damn shame he wouldn't have the spending of all that money, after being broke so long!

Oh well, as long as there was nothing of Nelle's in the place.

He looked at his watch. Fourteen minutes to the rebroadcast.

He gave the room one last, hurried look, saw that he had left no trace of his own visit, left the door slightly ajar just as he had found it, and raced to his waiting taxi.

"—and step on it, fella!"

The driver nodded, shot down the street, and immediately became hopelessly embroiled in a traffic jam.

Where was Nelle Brown?

Jake Justus cursed himself as the stupidest of all stupid fools. Why hadn't he gone there to look for her in the first place? Why hadn't he managed to find her, wherever she had gone? Or, failing to find her, why hadn't he gone back to the studio and arranged for a double for the rebroadcast?

Now they would all be in the soup, unless someone had had sense enough to rise to the occasion, which he doubted. Again he took out his watch. Six minutes now. What would they do? Probably throw in a substitute program of sorts, and the sponsor, dear Mr. Goldman, would have a litter of leopards. Hell would be calm and quiet compared to what was going to pop. How was he ever going to get Nelle out of this mess?

The taxi dumped him out at the door with less than a minute to go.

He raced across the lobby, dived into a waiting elevator, and gasped, "Late. Nelle Brown rebroadcast."

The elevator operator, used to emergencies, nodded, slammed the door, and the car shot upward without a stop.

The elevator stopped at the studio floor and Jake stepped into the reception room just as someone turned on the loud-speaker. A voice, warm and rich and dramatic, calm as a lake at early evening, and absolutely unmistakable, filled the room.

"Golden Moon . . . over the midnight sky. . . ."

Relief flooded over him in a great, almost unbearable wave. He leaned against the wall a moment, catching his breath.

Of all the silly things to have imagined! Just because one of Nelle

Brown's ex-sweeties managed to get himself shot, he'd practically had Nelle strapped in the electric chair. The idea of Nelle Brown murdering anybody! She probably hadn't even been near the place.

He slipped into the control room, mopping his brow. Schultz grinned sympathetically, waved him into one of the uncomfortable black-leather-and-chromium-piped chairs.

There she was, standing beside Bob Bruce the announcer, her face up-turned, singing. There was not a tremor, not even the faintest suggestion of a tremor, in her voice.

Wherever she had gone between broadcasts, she had returned safely and in plenty of time. Not one shining wave of her golden-brown hair was disturbed; her exquisite, flowerlike face—though as pale as it had been before—was newly powdered. Her deep-rose dress was fresh and unwrinkled.

But her handkerchief!

Her immense, pale-green chiffon handkerchief that she passed nervously through her hands as she sang had an ugly stain in one corner.

It had not been there when she left the studio.

Even through the heavy glass of the control-room window, Jake Justus could see that it was blood.

CHAPTER 3

Jake told the taxi driver to go around Grant Park until further orders, and to close the glass partition. Then he turned to Nelle, huddled in a corner. "Paul March had it coming to him, but why did you do it?"

"I don't know what you're talking about," she said sullenly.

He carefully unfolded the green chiffon handkerchief across her knee so that the stain showed darkly. She snatched it back from sight.

"What did you do with the gun, Nelle? I hope to heaven you pitched it in the river."

"I never had a gun. I didn't shoot him."

He swore wearily and at length, without repeating himself.

"Jake, please believe me."

"I don't give a damn if you shot him or not. My job is to keep you out of trouble, and I'm going to do it. Don't forget your contract is up for re-signing. It's none of my business whether or not you shot the guy, but will you please tell me where you got the gun and what you did with it, and who might have seen you going there, so I'll know just what I've got to do first?"

"But I didn't shoot him, Jake. You've got to believe me. I was there tonight, yes. That's right. But I didn't shoot him."

"You said that before," he said glumly.

"I went there. I'd written him some letters, last winter."

Jake asked, "Just how bad were they?"

"Well—pretty warm. He was a—oh, skip that. Anyway, he kept them. I should have known this was coming when he called up and tried to borrow money from me."

"Did he succeed?" Jake asked interestedly.

Her answer was brief, vituperative, and profane.

"Well," he said mildly, "I didn't think you would."

"I don't mind loaning money to a friend, but not to a skunk. Not after the way he treated me."

"I don't blame you," Jake said, "but go on. He had your letters. He tried to borrow money from you. Take it up from there."

"Jake, I said I should have seen this coming. Anyway, I heard from him today. He sent me a note. Offered to sell me the letters. You can imagine," she said with feeling, "just what would happen if Tootz should ever know about this."

"Tootz," Jake said, "or your adoring public."

"Oh, the hell with the public. Can't you think of anything else at a time like this? Well anyway, Jake, I wasn't going to kick in, not to that rat. I was going up there between shows and scare the everlasting God-damned living daylights out of him, and get my letters back without giving him a dime. I'd have done it too," she added thoughtfully, "if some bastard hadn't gotten there first and shot him."

Jake said scornfully, "Who would want to shoot him?"

"Who wouldn't?" Nelle asked, just as scornfully.

He tried to think of an answer to that one, couldn't, and asked instead, "What did you do with the letters?"

"I didn't do anything with them. I didn't find them."

"What do you mean, you couldn't find them?"

"I said what you heard. They weren't there."

He murmured, "Good God!" under his breath, and snapped his cigarette out the cab window.

"Jake darling, I looked everywhere. I did everything but tear the paper off the walls. Those letters weren't anywhere in the place."

"But it don't make sense," he said stupidly.

"Either he hadn't really kept them and was just trying to bluff me, or else somebody else has them now."

Jake inquired loudly of an unanswering and possibly disinterested providence why he had ever taken on the job of managing Nelle Brown.

Just the same, he looked at her with reluctant admiration. Between broadcasts she had gone to bluff a blackmailer into giving back the foolish letters she had written him, and had found the man dead. She had walked into what must have been an agonizingly familiar room and stumbled on the murdered body of a man she had been wildly in love with only a few months before. (Or had she found him alive and left him dead?) Whatever had happened, she had done a magnificent job of the rebroadcast, as smooth as though nothing, not even the most trivial thing, had disturbed her.

Nelle Brown chose that moment to hurl herself at his shoulder, bury her head in it, and begin to cry, noisily and childishly.

"He used to be so sweet to me, Jake. Just sweet. Good-for-nothing louse if there ever was one. Can't you imagine what it was like, walking in there tonight? It was wintertime when—remember? I used to stop in there and he'd have a fire going in the fireplace, and he always took my galoshes off for me, and I'd watch the snow going down past the window. Everything looked just the way it always did, with the little chromium ash tray on the end table, the one we got with cigarette coupons. And he was there on the kitchen floor, dead. All bloody, Jake. I used to be so happy with him. Remember how awful it was when Joe McIvers had him fired, and he told me that it was all just so he'd get the job of producing the show? He hadn't really cared about me, he just wanted my show to do. Remember how you sat up with me for three nights in a row, and how we thought I'd never get sobered up for rehearsal, and that terrible Turkish-bath place you took me to? I could have sworn he was in love with me. Oh, Jake, he couldn't have said some of the things he said and not meant them."

Jake held her very gently for a few minutes and let her talk on and on, until at last she sat bolt upright and said in a calm, perfectly clear voice, "I wonder where in hell those letters are now."

He looked at her and shook his head wearily. No, he would never quite understand her. No one ever would.

"And all that money, Jake. Where did he get all that money? I didn't give it to him."

"Somebody did," Jake said thoughtfully. "Why? Nobody would lend him that much." He considered it for a minute, and said, "He sold the letters to somebody else. Or he was blackmailing somebody else and somebody shot him. Or—but why shoot him and then not take the money back?"

He sighed. "He was blackmailing somebody we will call A, and some-body we will call B came in and shot him. This gets too damned compli-cated, Nelle. You must have shot him yourself."

"Go to hell!"

He said slowly, "Aside from the problem of the letters, you may have been seen going there tonight. Or somebody may remember you used to spend a lot of time with him last winter. I jumped to the conclusion you'd shot him the minute I saw him, and it's just possible, baby, a jury of twelve good men may jump to the same conclusion."

"No, Jake! Oh no!"

"It does happen to people," he told her calmly. "And even if that even-tually doesn't come about, you may still get messed up in a nasty, sordid murder case, and you know what happens to people in radio when they get into things like that. Remember what happened to Annette just be-cause she was named as correspondent in a very ugly divorce action. Swell little actress, Annette, and not a director in town will touch her with a ten-foot pole."

"I know," she said reflectively. "I paid Annette's rent for her last week, and only God knows what she's eating on."

"Well," he said, "there's an old, old saying, baby. It might have hap-pened to you."

"And Tootz," she said, her voice suddenly strained and harsh. "Tootz. If he knew. Oh, Jake, that would be awful. Jake, that mustn't happen."

"It may, when the police start nosing around in their horrid, inquisitive way," Jake told her.

"Jake, I shouldn't have called the police when I found him, should I?"

He leaned back against the cushions and talked emphatically to heaven about Nelle Brown.

"Hell," she said, "nobody could be that stupid, at least I know I'm not."

"The police will find out about it soon enough," he said, "and without our help, too. Just pray they don't learn that either of us dropped in there tonight, and you also might pray that whoever has those letters is a friend of yours."

"What do you mean, Jake?"

"I mean that conceivably somebody murdered March for them in order to do the blackmailing himself. In which case this affair might run into money."

"Money," Nelle Brown said scornfully. "Who the devil cares about money?"

He reminded her briefly and untactfully that there had been days when she would have sold the flowers off her grandmother's grave for the price of a cup of coffee and a hamburger.

She ignored him, and said, "But if whoever has those letters is a friend of mine—"

"Then Paul March may have been murdered to get you out of a jam." He looked at his watch. "Listen, baby. We'll cope with those things later. Right now, you've got to go to Max's. Everybody from the show is going there, and you're expected. You've got to give the impression that you don't know what's happened. Does Tootz think you're coming home to-night?"

"No."

"Date with Baby?"

"Yes."

"Well, when Baby shows up, send him home as soon as you can. I'm not going to let you out of my sight until this breaks." He tapped on the glass, told the driver to take them to Max's. "I'll get you out of this some-how, but you've got to do exactly as I tell you, every blessed minute."

"I will, Jake."

He felt agreeably sure he could depend on that.

At Max's, he paused a moment in the doorway. "Chase up to the little girl's room and wash your face. I'll be waiting for you right here. For the love of Pete, hide that damn handkerchief until you get a chance to burn it."

"Yes, Jake." Her voice seemed almost too docile.

Jake decided to stop worrying. Luckily, Max's was the best place for her to be seen tonight. It was a comfortable, informal, noisy restaurant and bar, where the cast of the Nelle Brown Revue usually gathered after the show. Everyone would remember that Nelle Brown had been there; everyone would remember that she had been her usual lighthearted self. (He hoped!)

Oscar Jepps paused on his way to the bar. "Where the hell have you two been all this time?"

"Riding around Grant Park in a taxi," Jake said.

Oscar laughed appreciatively, shaking a collection of chins. "That's very funny."

There was nothing, Jake reflected, like telling the truth if you wanted to get a reputation as a wit.

Then Nelle returned, no sign of tears on her serene face. The pale-green handkerchief was stuck outrageously through her bracelet, innocent of any stain.

"Washed it," she whispered impishly.

They were greeted by an uproar of welcome from one end of the big room. There was much confusion in rearranging tables, shifting chairs, and ordering drinks, but when everyone had settled down again, Jake was right at Nelle's side, where he had intended to be.

He sipped his rye slowly and looked around the room. You couldn't, he reflected, heave a brick in any direction without hitting a radio artist. (And why not?) There was Bob Bruce, big and blond and handsome (his good-looking face was the trial of his life). McIvers, looking as though he never got enough sleep (he never did); Lou Silver, a little, shiny-haired man, showing off before a heavily mascaraed brunette; a stranger with glasses and a red mustache (they never did find out who he was); the pale, fastidious, Boston-accented John St. John and his homely, brown-haired wife who could be such amazingly good fun (Jake remembered the week end of Oscar's house party and had the grace to blush); a rather nice-looking blonde in a tight blue dress, and, on the other side of Nelle, the inevitable Baby.

There was, to Jake, a curious unreality about it all. There was the usual talk, the usual patter, the usual drinking, the usual attempts to put Essie St. John under the table. While only six or eight blocks away there was that crumpled body on a kitchen floor. He remembered how many times the man who lay dead had been with them at Max's, with everyone trying to be nice to him for Nelle's sake. Last year's Baby, Jake thought grimly.

He looked slowly around the table. Had one of them slipped over to that shabby apartment between broadcasts and killed a man? But which one of them, and why?

Or had it been Nelle after all?

CHAPTER 4

How did you get to be a radio star?" the red-haired stranger was asking Nelle.

One of the penalties of being a radio star, Jake reflected, was that everyone asked you how you got to be that way.

Nelle simpered ever so slightly, and said, "Well, I used to sing in the choir in the little Nebraska town where I was brought up, and one day—"

"Hell's bells," Oscar growled, "couldn't Jake write you a better story than that?"

"He has," John St. John said dispassionately, "several, in fact. Why don't you write the true one someday?"

Jake grinned and said, "I might," and wondered what would happen if he ever did. Nelle had been the daughter of a cheap entertainer in a fifth-rate dive. A few years in public school and a ratty home in a one-room basement apartment from which she was chased to the neighborhood movie whenever her mother had "company" constituted her childhood and education.

"How did you get into show business?" the red-haired stranger persisted.

Nelle looked him straight in the eye and told him she had been born backstage and had played little Eva at the age of six. The red-haired stranger looked interested but skeptical, and Jake remembered that Nelle had been adopted by the boss of a traveling medicine show at the age of twelve. He had seen pictures of her: a thin, rather attractive, leggy child, with a mass of curly hair, and immense, hungry eyes. Two years later, professing to be sixteen, she had turned up in the chorus of a second-rate burlesque company.

A long way from that to the Nelle Brown Revue. Jake sighed deeply, ordered another rye, and reflected that if this murder story broke the wrong way, Nelle would zigzag right back to a second-rate burlesque company.

"Let's not talk about me," Nelle was telling the red-haired stranger, her eyes wide and dewy. "Let's talk about you."

The tableful of Nelle's friends cheered raucously, and the stranger lapsed into a discouraged silence.

"The truth is," Oscar Jepps said, "when Nelle was seventeen she got to be a movie extra, and that's how the whole thing started."

He neglected to add that when Nelle was seventeen her life included some five years in more-or-less dubious show business and a marriage that had ended abruptly when her husband shot it out with the police of Kansas City. But the curious stranger appeared to be satisfied.

John St. John chose that particular moment to ask, "Did you ever find your script, Nelle?"

Nelle gave several minutes to discussing the undiluted whatsisname who could have stolen her script out of the studio before the broadcast, making it necessary for her to mark up another one at the last minute. She implied that whoever would have done such a thing had a maternal parent who was African, illiterate, unwashed, and unwed.

The red-haired stranger looked a little startled.

John St. John lifted his left eyebrow a trifle and muttered something about the inexcusable carelessness of leaving a script in the studio. Jake repressed an impulse to ask him whether his pale hair had been parted by an architectural draftsman or a certified public accountant.

Someone sent for another round of drinks.

The mascaraed brunette leaned across the table and asked, "Miss Brown, didn't you used to sing with Dick Dayton's band?"

Nelle nodded. "Almost a year. That's where I met Jake, he was managing Dayton. Dayton was a big success and I was a big success, and so we split up."

McIvers broke his usual morose silence. "Eighteen months ago I had Nelle all ready to sign on the dotted line. Her own show, her own name headlined, and enough money every week to choke a horse. And then she went and got married." He looked sadly into his glass.

Jake wondered why so many agency account executives appeared to have been marked by some great personal tragedy. The only real tragedy he knew of in Joe McIvers' life was that his pet sponsor, Papa Goldman, liked to fish, and Joe didn't.

The red-haired stranger whispered to him confidentially, "Miss Brown is married?"

Jake nodded. "Henry Gibson Gifford."

The stranger's eyes grew appreciative. "Socialite millionaire. I know who he is."

"Not a millionaire any more," Jake reminded him.

The stranger looked meditative. "Sixty, isn't he?"

"Young in heart," Jake said, wishing the man would go away.

"Talking about Tootz?" Oscar Jepps asked amiably, taking his plump hand off the arm of the blonde in blue.

Jake nodded and wished the red-haired stranger onto Oscar.

"Handsomest man of his age or any age in the city of Chicago," he heard Oscar mumbling. "Best-dressed man in America. Most beautifully tended white hair and mustache in the civilized world."

Jake recalled a bright-eyed and glowing Nelle confiding in him that Henry (though even then she called him Tootz) was so sweet, and she adored him. Of course she was marrying him for his money. She'd be a fool not to, wouldn't she? But he was such a lamb. She'd want to marry him if he didn't have a dime in the world. Jake had told her at the time that she could think up the sweetest stories.

Oscar was explaining to the red-haired stranger that Nelle would probably never have returned to radio if Gifford and Company hadn't failed, leaving Tootz with nothing except the shirt on his back, and a mortgage on that.

"But didn't Henry Gibson Gifford lose his mind after the crash?" the red-mustached stranger asked in a whisper perfectly audible two blocks away. Three people managed to kick him under the table as he reached the last word.

"He has delusions," Oscar murmured. The shadow of a grin crossed his cheerful, moonlike face.

Everyone began talking about the night's broadcast.

Five drinks later, the red-haired stranger remembered something he had wanted to ask Nelle for a long time.

"How did you get to be a radio star?"

At that point Nelle was warmed up to answering, "I'll tell you, if you'll tell me how you got to be such a dope."

The stranger was squelched again.

The party went on talking about the broadcast. Jake found he was pleasantly able to answer questions and remarks without annoying his mind about what he was saying. He heard St. John's chilly voice address the young man next to Nelle as "Baby" and noticed the frown that crossed the young man's face.

He felt a little sorry for Baby. What the hell was his real name, anyway? Oh yes, Macy McKee. No wonder Nelle called him Baby. A little different from the usual men in Nelle's life. Young—a little too young for Nelle, he thought—a newcomer to Chicago from somewhere in the East. Not a bad actor, either. Oscar had praised his work, and no one was a better judge. Well, his affair with Nelle would give him a chance to show what talent he had. By the time it broke up, he ought to be established as an actor. Jake wondered if the boy knew that.

That reminded him of the current mess Nelle was in.

"Don't forget to chase Baby home," he whispered to her.

She nodded, and about three drinks later the young man was gone.

From Jake's point of view, it was not a successful party. Perhaps, he told himself, because he was staying too sober. Or perhaps because he was trying to pick a likely murder suspect from the group around the table.

He managed a warning glance at Nelle, cleared his throat ever so little, and asked casually, "Anyone here seen Paul March lately?"

For an instant it was as though mass paralysis had struck the party. (Though, he decided later, that might have been shock at his tactlessness in mentioning Paul March in front of Nelle.)

In the breath of time before several people murmured, "No," and sev-

eral others hastily changed the subject, he thought that Essie St. John,
Oscar Jepps, Joe McIvers, St. John and the red-mustached stranger all
turned pale and looked guilty. He wondered if he'd turned pale and looked
guilty himself.

The only positive decision he reached was that it was a damn silly idea
to bother to stay sober, murder or no murder. He sighed, relaxed, ordered
a double rye, and wished he was back press-agenting Dick Dayton and his
dance band.

Oscar Jepps began insulting McIvers. Oscar always had to insult someone to feel happy; he claimed it was the great producer in him coming to
the surface. Everyone knew him as the gentlest and kindest-hearted man
alive and besides, no one as fat as Oscar Jepps could be really insulting.
McIvers took it gloomily but nicely; everyone always insulted him just as
a matter of course. It was like the Armenians, Jake thought, people were
always massacring them because it seemed so suitable. There were some
disconsolate individuals who were born to be abused; they either grew up
to be Armenians or account executives in advertising agencies. Joe McIvers
always perspired and achieved a deeply apologetic air when insulted.

Jake remembered suddenly that Joe McIvers hadn't attended the rebroadcast. That was funny. He wondered where he had been.

John St. John wandered upstairs and lost twenty dollars in a crap game.
Everyone was secretly delighted. While he was gone, Essie St. John made
a date with Bob Bruce, and everyone pretended not to hear. The blonde in
the tight blue dress asked Jake how she could get a job in radio, and gave
him her telephone number, which he promptly lost. The red-mustached
stranger upset his drink across the table.

It was exactly like every other evening at Max's that Jake could remember. Except that one man who had spent so many evenings at Max's lay
dead behind the dingy green curtains of a little kitchenette.

The heavily mascaraed brunette slapped Lou Silver, probably with good
reason, and left the table. Lou chased after her, and Oscar remarked that
Lou Silver spent half his time chasing women.

"Ever catch any?" the stranger asked.

Oscar spotted Lou coming back alone, and said, "No."

Lou played the out-of-tune piano and Nelle sang requests for everybody in the place. (A thousand or so a week for one program, Jake thought,
and she'd sing all night for anyone who bought her a drink.)

Eventually, to his great relief, it was time to go home. There was the
usual confusion over who was going where in whose car; in the midst of
it he managed to get Nelle away without anyone noticing that they left

together. Not that anyone would have cared. She muttered something about her fate being in his hands, curled up with her head on his lap, and went to sleep.

A sudden idea came to Jake, and he told the driver to go down Erie Street, slowly. Damned fool thing to do, he told himself. But he was curious. He wanted to see just what kind of a rumpus was going on at the scene of the murder.

There was no rumpus going on at all. No lights, no crowds on the sidewalk, no police cars in front of the long, low building. Nothing.

Was it possible the murder hadn't been discovered?

Evidently it was not only possible, but true. Well, it would come any minute now. He knew that building from away back; people went wandering in and out of other people's apartments all day and night. Sooner or later someone would wander into apartment 215.

A little later he deposited Nelle on the bed, covered her with a blanket, shaded the light from her face, and stood looking at her.

Nelle Brown. Her flaming rages when anything went wrong in rehearsal. Her spectacular language in anger, gleaned from years in burlesque companies, cheap night clubs, and God knows where. The quick recovery she made from the very worst of her rages. The intensely dramatic quality of her singing and acting. The way she bullied poor Joe McIvers at the agency. Escapades that all but turned Jake's red hair white, keeping her out of trouble. Her insane love affairs, always ending disastrously. Her honest friendliness and generosity, always good for a touch. Her sweetness and gentleness with Tootz, always bringing a curious tightness into Jake's throat.

Now, a mix-up in a murder case. She was, Jake reflected, just twenty-three years old! Lots more could still happen.

He poured himself a drink, turned his radio to the police calls, and sat listening.

"Car 117, go to 1219 Melvia Street, a disturbance in a tavern. W-P-B-D. Car 221, get a dog-bite report at 716 Marquise Avenue. Car 221, at 716 Marquise Avenue, a dog-bite report. W-P-B-D. Car 415, a suspicious man at the corner of—"

He poured himself another drink.

"W-P-B-D. Car 134, at the corner of State and Elm Streets, a policeman calling for assistance—"

"Officer, call a cop," Jake said happily, and went on listening.

"—and Wabash. Car 152, at Eighth and Wabash, a man lying on the sidewalk. W-P-B-D. Car 123, a cat is caught in a drainpipe at—"

After an hour he switched off the radio, reflected that he would read all about it in the morning papers. There was nothing he could do about it tonight anyway. He turned off the light and went to sleep in his chair.

CHAPTER 5

At eight o'clock in the morning, he sponged Nelle's face with a cold wet cloth until she blinked, opened her eyes, stared at him, and suddenly sat bolt upright.

"Jake. Last night. Something happened."

"A murder," he told her calmly, lighting a cigarette and putting it in her mouth.

She lay perfectly still for a long time, her face as impassive as the bottom of a bottle.

"We went to Max's. How did I get here?"

"Up the freight elevator. Over my shoulder, like a sack of potatoes."

"I don't believe it."

"Ask the bellhop. He always helps me carry my women up the freight elevator."

"I suppose it's the only way you can get them here," Nelle said reflectively and insultingly. She glanced at the rose taffeta dress. "I'd better phone for some clothes to go home in."

"I've already attended to that detail."

"You think of everything, don't you! What a manager!" She slid her feet off the bed, made a heroic effort to stand upright without wavering, finally succeeded, and shuddered. "But you never should have allowed those two Chinamen to commit suicide in my mouth."

"There's a new toothbrush in the bathroom and a jar of cold cream. The right kind, I hope. I went out and got them for you. Coffee and the morning papers are coming up. You'd better brace yourself for both with a shower bath."

"Yes, doctor. I'll be a new woman in five minutes." She paused lengthily, her face pale. "Jake. Jake, have you heard anything yet?"

He shook his head. "It'll all be in the papers, my pet. Go take your bath."

Coffee and the newspapers arrived as she emerged from the bathroom, her gold-brown hair damp and glistening, her face freshly powdered, her fragile body all but lost in Jake's bathrobe. He divided the coffee and newspapers equally between them.

A crisis in Europe. A divorce in Hollywood. Robbery of an alderman's wife. A vice probe in the suburbs. Disappearance of a high-school girl from Elkhart, Indiana. Several Congressional investigations. Two people killed in a traffic accident. Nothing else on page one.

"It's a front-page story," Jake muttered with professional contempt.

Nothing about the Erie Street murder, not on page two, page three, page four. Nothing in the entire paper. They went through the pages twice, three times, finally kicked the papers under the bed, and sat staring stupidly at each other.

"Jake, it can't *be*! They must have found him. Somebody must have found him. The door. You know. You said you left it ajar. Somebody would have gone in and found him. People go wandering around that building all the time. Especially when there's a party going on, and there was a party next door. Jake, I'm going crazy. *Do* something. Jake, somebody must have found him—"

"Shut up," Jake said. "I'll find out." He picked up the telephone called a number, and waited. "May I speak to Paul March?"

He held the receiver to his ear while Nelle paced the floor distractedly. "Evidently he hasn't been found yet. Landlady said she'd ring him." A long wait. "Hello? I wonder if you'd mind going up and waking him? It's very important." Again he sat holding the receiver, an even longer and more terrible wait.

"A dirty trick," Nelle said, "a very dirty trick to send her up there to find the body."

Jake said impatiently, "Well, God damn it, somebody's got to find— hello? Yes. Thank you. No, I'll call again." He put the telephone down very slowly and deliberately.

"Jake!"

"She says," Jake said very calmly, "that he isn't there. She says that he evidently didn't come home last night."

It was a long and an uncomfortable silence.

"But," Nelle said, and stopped. "But. No, it's not possible."

Jake lit a cigarette, walked to the window, and stood looking out. "Nelle, I've got to know now. The sensible thing, of course, is to sit tight and wait for developments. But I'm not going to do it."

"Jake, what are you going to do?"

"I don't know yet. Give me a little time."

He continued to stare moodily out the window.

The arrival of Nelle's maid with her clothes was a welcome diversion. Jake tactfully went downstairs for cigarettes he didn't need, and returned

fifteen minutes later to find Nelle a vision in pale-brown wool and vast
quantities of red fox. Her hair was smooth and shining over her shoulders;
she was crumpling a soft felt hat between her hands.

"Very nice," he said approvingly.

"Jake, you've got to do something. You've got to. I can't stand this."

"Oh yes you can. You've damned well got to stand it." He stood looking
at her for a long moment. How anybody so lovely and so fragile could get
mixed up in so damn many things. And now, murder. It wasn't fair, by
God, no it wasn't. All he wanted was a nice quiet life as a manager and a
press agent, and here he was with a chronic earthquake on his hands.

"You'd better go home," he said at last.

She nodded. "Tootz expected me hours ago. Probably he's worrying
himself crazy right now." She grinned wryly. "Or maybe I ought to say
he's worrying himself sane."

"Don't, Nelle." He winced.

"Don't you think it hurts me worse than it does you? Anyway, Tootz
isn't crazy. He's just a little different from other people."

"Just eccentric," Jake murmured.

She smiled at him, and then frowned. "Jake, who killed Paul March?"

"I don't know," Jake said, "but I hope you didn't."

He took her downstairs, put her in a taxi, and sent her on her way,
warning her to stay home, stay sober, and keep her chin up and her mouth
shut until she heard from him.

It was not far to the Erie Street address. He stood at the corner of Ohio
and Michigan, looking at the river of traffic going past, and decided to
walk. No sense in letting the world, or even one possibly inquisitive taxi
driver, know where he was going.

The day was warm and sunny and pleasant. Groups of laughing people
passed him on their way to the beach; smartly dressed and perfectly turned-
out men and women jostled others casually clad in beach robes, dressing
gowns, and pajamas. Jake passed a tennis court where brown-skinned young-
sters in shorts were making a big job of batting balls back and forth. Here and
there a few scraggly trees moved gently in the wind. It was a wonderful day,
a heavenly day, a marvelous day. And instead of strolling lazily in the sun,
watching the tennis players and the swimmers at Oak Street beach, he was
going to that shabby little one-room apartment, to find out why no one had
discovered the huddled body on the kitchen floor.

The apartment building was a group of remodeled dwellings that had
been made into one by the simple expedient of cutting doors through the
first-floor halls. The result was a perfect labyrinth of hallways, a con-

glomeration of odd-shaped apartments all the way from the attic to the basement, no two alike, old-fashioned bathrooms and temperamental plumbing, and an insane confusion of stairways. Including first floor, basement, and rear entrances, Jake had once totaled eleven different ways of getting into and out of the building. Yet it had an indescribably comfortable charm.

He thanked a provident heaven that few people were stirring in the halls. The inhabitants with jobs had already left; those without jobs were still asleep. He walked along the hall, went around two corners, and up a flight of stairs.

There was, he noticed, a tomblike silence in the apartment that had housed last night's riotous brawl.

At the door to Paul March's apartment, he paused. He was, he decided, being either very smart or very dumb. It was going to be difficult to explain his presence, if someone happened to walk in and find him there. If someone happened to be in there right now, it was going to be just as difficult to explain his arrival.

He knocked on the door, and waited.

No answer.

What in blazes was he going to do after he did go in? Make a noisy gesture of finding the body? Dash down to the lobby yelling, "Murder!" Explain that he had come to see Paul March, and found him dead?

Explain how he, Jake Justus, press agent and manager of Nelle Brown, was going to see Paul March—when everyone in town (save Tootz, Mr. Goldman, and the general public) knew all the details of last winter's March-Brown affair?

Or it was going to look very silly to stroll down to the lobby and say to the landlady, "Look here, there's been a murder up in 215, and you ought to report it to the police." Just like that, as though he were reporting the unwelcome presence of a cockroach in the kitchen sink.

What possible good was it going to do to go in that room, take a look at the remains of Paul March, and go away again? The chances were Nelle was completely in the clear. No one could have seen her going to the apartment last night. No one was going to involve her in this. The thing to do was to go quietly away and forget about it.

Having reached that sensible decision, Jake tried the door. It was still unlocked. He pushed it open slowly and stood in the little hallway for a moment. The light had been turned off, probably by the landlady when she went to call Paul March to the telephone. But if she had gone into the room, she would have discovered the murder. No, she couldn't have gone in. Then who had turned off the light?

There was an unpleasant coolness in the exact center of his stomach.

Slowly and very quietly he went in. Everything looked just as it had been the night before.

Then he looked toward the kitchen.

No, everything was not as it had been the night before.

The kitchen linoleum was clean and shining and unspotted, newly washed. The huddled body of Paul March was gone.

CHAPTER 6

Jake stopped in at the little bar on the corner and ordered a double rye. He needed it. Then he strolled over to Michigan Avenue and began walking north, hardly conscious of where he was going.

What the hell!

There was this way of looking at it. Now that the body of Paul March had disappeared, there wasn't the same chance of Nelle being involved in a nasty murder case. The body might turn up again somewhere else, but this would give him a little time.

A fine thing, with Nelle's contract up for renewal. *If* the body had been found, and *if* Nelle had been seen going to the building last night, and *if* she'd been fool enough to tell anyone that March was blackmailing her—! But, he thanked his stars, it hadn't been found.

What the devil had happened to the body of Paul March?

Of course, it wouldn't have been hard to smuggle a body out of that building. It wouldn't be hard to smuggle an elephant out of there, especially with a party going on. But where was the body now? What had been the idea of taking it away? And when would it be found?

There was an amusing possibility that it never would be, and no one would ever know Paul March had been murdered. No one save three people: Nelle, the unknown murderer, and himself. Jake conceded to himself that this might be two people. Of course, the disappearance would make some stir. After all, Jake reflected, the man must have had some friends. It was a cinch he had had some creditors. Anyway, there was the landlady to make inquiries. But a disappearance was hardly the same as murder.

Suppose no one ever knew!

All right, Jake thought, suppose no one ever did. It was no skin off his nose. Murder, as such, didn't worry him. This wasn't his murder, and he didn't want to make it his. But Nelle was a valuable property, far too valuable to be destroyed. This might be profitable publicity in some other branch of the entertainment world. But not in radio. Oh no, Jake thought, not in radio! One good strong breath of scandal and Nelle's value would drop to zero overnight. He'd seen it happen to too many others.

He speculated calmly on the possibility of Nelle as the murderer. If she had been, though, who had moved the body? Not Nelle, he'd been with her every minute since the rebroadcast.

His mind moved on to the next problem. Where were Nelle's letters? This was a far more serious menace than an obligingly disappearing corpse.

He decided that it was something he couldn't cope with himself, and a name popped into his mind. John Joseph Malone.

Merely thinking of the name made him feel that the whole problem was a simple one, already half solved. John Joseph Malone, untidy, resource-ful little criminal lawyer, who boasted that he could get anybody out of any mess. He could certainly get Nelle Brown out of this one.

Jake remember how John Joseph Malone, whom he had known from his first days as a reporter, had turned up the real murderer of Miss Alex-andria Inglehart of Maple Park and exonerated the murdered woman's niece, Dick Dayton's bride. That had been a tough one, even for Malone. (Though the lawyer still insisted that if Holly Inglehart Dayton had been brought to trial, he could have won an acquittal on the first ballot with an insanity defense.)

The thought of Malone brought another name to mind, and the shadow of a frown crossed his lean face.

Helene Brand! Was there another woman in the world like Helene Brand? She had wandered into the Inglehart case, a childhood friend of Holly, and had gone through it to the cockeyed end.

For a very long time now, he had tried not to think of Helene Brand. All during the Inglehart case he had tried to find time to carry out some very important and quite dishonorable intentions he had regarding her. Then when the case was closed, he had suddenly realized he wanted to marry her.

Insane and impossible idea! Helene Brand of Maple Park, famous beauty, socialite, heiress. Jake Justus of downtown Chicago, ex-reporter, man-ager, promoter, press agent, who would never amount to a damn. Yet, realizing her importance to him, he knew that he could not make casual love to her. That had been what she seemed to expect and—thoroughly disgusted with him, no doubt—she had vanished. Oh, it was probably just as well. He could see now that he hadn't meant anything to her. Just an escapade, a mad moment in the life of an heiress. Nuts!

It had been nearly a year and a half ago. He remembered telling Nelle,

in the worst stages of her heartbreak over Paul March, that time took care
of everything in its own way. Well, time hadn't seemed to make much
impression on his memories of Helene Brand.

Why the devil couldn't he forget her anyway? He would never see her
again.

But he knew it was the image of Helene Brand that kept him from making love to Nelle Brown, as Lou Silver, and Schultz, and Oscar, and nearly
everyone connected with the program had done or tried to do. The delicately sculptured face of Helene Brand would always superimpose itself
on any face he tried to kiss. The silvery, mocking laughter of Helene Brand
would always drown out any lovely voice that called to him.

He reminded himself that he was not going to think of Helene Brand,
and with a wrenching effort brought his mind back to today, to now, to
Nelle Brown, the Nelle Brown Revue, and the murder of Paul March.

John Joseph Malone would handle it. Malone would find a way.

Jake passed Chicago Avenue, passed a group of chattering bathers bound
for Oak Street beach, noticed Chicago's Best-Dressed Woman crossing
Michigan Avenue, and paused for a moment by the old water tower, gaz-
ing at the Palmolive Building as it stood, sharp and clear, against a blazing
blue sky. He had seen it a thousand times before—veiled by snow, brilliant in the sunlight, or blurred by summer rain—but this time he paused
to gaze and admire, letting the combination of gray stone and intense blue
sky drive the worries of the moment from his tired mind.

In that moment a wonderfully familiar voice spoke just behind him.

"It looks just the way it does on the post cards!"

He wheeled around, knowing he couldn't mistake that mocking drawl,
not daring to believe it. It was true. Helene Brand!

There she stood, as patrician, as beautiful, as perfect as ever, in the
midst of the noontime crowds on Michigan Avenue. Her pale blond hair
was exquisitely in place, and she was dressed simply in a very low-cut
pale-violet chiffon evening gown. She was carrying a Parma violet evening
wrap. And she was not sober.

"Well!" said Jake Justus inadequately. "Well! Imagine meeting you here!"

CHAPTER 7

Hello, baby," Jake Justus said tenderly.

The exquisite blonde girl on the bed moaned, stirred, sat up. For a moment she sat there blinking, looking around the disordered room: a half-empty bottle on the dresser, an overturned ash tray on the floor, her evening wrap fastened gracefully around the bridge lamp in the corner, and Jake Justus in the easy chair by the window, surrounded by a squirrel's nest of newspapers.

"Hello, baby," he said again.

"Well, well, well. Here we are again." She yawned and stretched. "What was the crack Malone made once about life being a bum phonograph record that kept slipping back and playing the same groove? My life, anyway." She yawned again.

Jake said, "There's something about history repeating itself. Seems like I read it somewhere, in a book. So first I get mixed up in a murder, and then I run into you."

"Murder," she said, laughing politely. "That's very funny."

"It is very funny," Jake told her, "because that's what happened. And Malone is on his way here right now."

She stared at him: "You couldn't be telling me the truth, by any chance?"

"I could be," Jake said, "and I am. How do you feel?"

She shuddered.

"I imagine so," he said reflectively. "Where were you, or do you know, or does it matter?"

"A party," she told him. "It's probably still going on if you'd like to go. I didn't like any of the people, so I went for a walk and I met you."

"Nice dress," he said. "Pretty color."

She nodded. "Yes, it is. Tell me about this murder."

"Later," he said.

"How did I get here?"

"You went to sleep," Jake said. "On the corner of Michigan and Chicago Avenues. I brought you up the freight elevator. Helene, have you missed me?"

"Terribly," she said. "Tell me, Jake, whom did you murder, and why?"

"I didn't murder him," Jake said, "and I hope my client didn't. Where have you been since I saw you last?"

"Florida," she said, "and Paris and Lake Geneva and Wyoming. Who is your client, and who was murdered?"

"Nelle Brown," Jake told her. "You've heard her. Nelle Brown's Revue. Why did you disappear the way you did?"

"I'll tell you why sometime. Nelle Brown's good. I like to listen to her. Whom did she murder?"

"Maybe she didn't murder anybody," Jake said, "but somebody did, only the body's missing. Have you been having a good time?"

"Wonderful," she said, "and stick to one subject, damn you. Who was murdered, and if Nelle Brown didn't do it, who did, and how do you know anyone was murdered if you can't find the body?"

Before Jake had a chance to wrestle with that one, John Joseph Malone arrived.

The famous criminal lawyer was a short, plumpish, untidy little man, with disturbed black hair, and a round red face that always grew rounder and redder with agitation. At the moment he had been celebrating the acquittal of a charming young woman who had shot her husband, and as the case had been a difficult one, complicated by the fact that her husband had been a police officer, he was red-eyed and tired. He was not surprised to see Helene Brand. Nothing ever surprised John J. Malone.

"Give me a drink," he said, sitting down in the most comfortable chair and dropping an inch of cigar ash on his vest. "I got her off. Uncovered enough monkeydoodling going on in the police department so that I could talk to all the brother officers of the deceased—persuade them, so to speak—to get up and testify that he was an unmitigated sonofabitch who deserved shooting. He was, too. It was no perjury." He looked at Helene. "Where did you find her?"

Jake told him, and poured three drinks.

"Now," Helene said, "now that Malone is here, maybe you'll give out about this murder of yours."

Jake scowled into his rye. "I can't prove that there was a murder," he said slowly, "because the body's lost. But Nelle saw it, and I saw it, and I'd be convinced that she did it, except that she told me she didn't, and she wouldn't have any reason for lying to me about it."

Malone sighed heavily and gloomily. "It would make life a lot simpler if you'd stay sober when you have something to tell me."

"I am sober," Jake said indignantly, emptying the glass of rye down his throat. "And there was a body, and it is lost."

"All right, all right," Malone said, "I believe you. But begin at the beginning."

Jake began at the beginning and told them the whole story: Nelle's affair with Paul March and its unhappy ending, the attempt at blackmail, the discovery of the body and its subsequent disappearance. He told it glowingly and with feeling, and ended his narrative by refilling the glasses all around.

"A very pretty little tale," Malone said, "and credible, too. Now let's all go out and buy a drink somewhere."

"Damn you, Malone," Jake said indignantly, "this is serious."

"Murder is always serious," Malone said, spilling a little rye on his necktie. "That's why they execute people for it. But what do you want me to do about this one? If it's your conscience that bothers you, tell it to a policeman, not to me." He reached for the bottle. "If this Paul March was the kind of a dope you just described, shooting him must have been the best idea someone ever had. We might even hunt up the guy and buy him a drink."

Jake lost his temper, drained his glass, and shouted, "I'm thinking about Nelle. Nelle, Nelle, Nelle, Nelle, NELLE."

"You sound like something by the late Edgar A. Poe," Helene observed.

"What about Nelle?" Malone said disgustedly. "The Body's disappeared and it may never be found."

"You know that isn't true," Jake said. "It's bound to turn up sooner or later. You can't just go out and lose a corpse."

"People do," Malone said philosophically. "But suppose it does turn up? As long as it doesn't turn up in that particular apartment, there's nothing to link Nelle Brown with the murder. Even if it is discovered that the murder occurred when and where it did, between the two of you, you and Nelle can fix up an alibi for the whole evening. By your own story, rehearsals and broadcasts took up most of the evening. Fix up something for the time between broadcasts, and she's completely in the clear."

Jake considered this a minute. "Where should I say we were in the time between broadcasts?"

Malone made a suggestion which Jake received with cold disfavor.

"Well anyway," Malone said confidently, "if some miracle should come along, and she were involved, I could get her out of it. You should let me tell you about my last case."

"Another time," Jake said, waving him silent. "It isn't just a question of keeping her out of the jug. Have you any vague idea of how moral radio is? Goldman would cancel her contract in a minute if this thing broke the wrong way. She'd be all washed up. Radio goes into the home; you've got to keep it clean." He poured another drink all around. "I know a guy, good announcer, got picked up in a raid on some South Side dive, and he hasn't been able to get a job since. Nice fella, too." He looked sadly into his glass.

"Look here, Jake," Helene asked, "suppose Nelle Brown really did shoot this guy."

"She'd still sound good on the air," Jake said.

Malone said, "Maybe she did shoot him. She had plenty of time and opportunity. She must have gone there right after the broadcast."

Jake nodded. "I phoned everywhere else. Even phoned her apartment, but no one answered."

The little lawyer mopped his red face. "She's got nothing to worry about even if she did the murder. If the police find the body, there's nothing to link the murder up with Nelle Brown. Nobody's going to run to the cops with the dope that she used to spend her spare time with the stiff, months back. If worst came to the worst, you could keep it out of the papers. What the hell has she got a press agent for?"

"You forget the letters," Jake said.

"Letters? Letters-letters-letters?"

"Hers to Paul March," Jake said. He added slowly, "I don't know who has them. But I'd guess the same person who murdered March."

Helene nodded sagely. "That makes sense. Someone knew he had the letters and murdered him for them."

"You catch on."

"You're both full of hop," Malone growled. "There might have been fifty other people who had fifty other reasons for murdering Paul March, and none of them anything to do with the letters."

"If it was one of them," Jake asked mildly, "where are the letters now and why are they missing?"

"Nelle did find them on her visit there, and destroyed them," the lawyer hazarded.

"Then why lie to me about it?" Jake demanded. "If she'd found the letters and destroyed them, I'm the first person she'd tell."

"Perhaps March had the letters hidden somewhere."

"We searched the apartment. Both of us. Everything but taking up the floor."

"He had them hidden somewhere away from the apartment, possibly in a safety-deposit box somewhere."

"But if he planned to sell the letters to Nelle, he'd have them at the apartment," Jake objected.

Malone groaned. "All right, damn it, I won't argue with you. He was murdered for Nelle Brown's letters." He paused for thought. "Someone else wants to blackmail Nelle and knows the value of those letters. Or someone who is a pal of Nelle's knew about the letters and knew that March was blackmailing her, and killed him and took the letters. Who would think enough of Nelle to do that for her?"

"Tootz," Jake said, "only he never knew anything about March, and he's nuts anyway. Baby, but he never knew anything about March either.

Lou Silver the band leader, Bob Bruce the announcer, McIvers who handles her program, Oscar Jepps the producer, Schultz the engineer, and myself."

"Did you murder him?" Malone asked.

"I considered it, but I was a little late."

"Still," Malone said, "if someone did it to protect Nelle, she'd get the letters back somehow. They'd be sent to her. Or she'd hear something."

"Maybe she has," Jake said. "I haven't seen her since morning."

"Morning?" Helene said inquiringly.

"I didn't want her to go home in the state of mind she was in, so I filled her up with Scotch at Max's, and the bellhop and I carried her up by the freight elevator."

"Two in a day," Helene commented. "I'd like to get the bellhop's opinion of you. What are we going to do, Malone?"

"There's two things we can do," John Joseph Malone said thoughtfully. "Both are risky. If we do nothing at all, someone may turn up with the letters and get Nelle into a new mess. If we find out who murdered March, we may involve her anyway. Providing," he added, "that we can find out who murdered him. And assuming," he finished, "that all this really happened and you weren't having delusions."

"I don't have delusions," Jake said indignantly. "It's Tootz that has delusions."

There was a long and meditative silence.

"But look," Helene said suddenly. "Why shoot a man, leave the body kicking around for some indeterminate length of time, and then come back, move the body, and wash the floor?"

"Maybe the murderer has naturally tidy instincts," Malone said.

Helene ignored him. "I'm curious."

"Find out who killed him," Jake said. "Maybe you'll get a client, Malone."

The lawyer snorted. "Find who murdered Paul March. No body. No proof there has been a murder. Nobody who even knows there's been a murder except you and Nelle Brown."

"One other," Jake reminded him. "The murderer."

"Unless it was you or Nelle," Malone said. "Find out where the body went, and why it went there, and who murdered him and how and why, and what was done with the letters and how to get them back safely, and then probably break our necks hushing up all we've dug up. Happy days!" He drank deeply. "We'll have to scare the birds out of the bushes and shoot them as they run."

"Fly," Helene corrected him.

After a long look out the window, the little lawyer said, "Let's go talk to Nelle Brown. That's the first move."

Helene remembered she had left her car in a Loop parking lot, they retrieved it and started north. On the way, Jake told Helene a little about Paul March, while Malone stared moodily over the lake. Paul March, Jake said, was a handsome lad and a brilliant one, but an unquestioned so-and-so. He had had some little success in radio, had managed a radio station in Iowa, been an announcer in Cincinnati, become an actor in Chicago, written thirteen weeks of a serial story, and finally advertised himself as a producer.

"The funny thing was," Jake said, "he was good. That was the hell of it. He used ways of getting jobs that I wouldn't mention in front of an innocent guy like Malone. Nelle was one of them. But he was good."

"I get an impression the man was attractive," Helene murmured.

"He could have charmed Diamond Lil out of a jewelry store," Jake assured her.

Helene sighed. "Too bad somebody shot him."

"You have me," he said consolingly. She patted his cheek and the big car missed a fire hydrant by inches.

"Don't forget not to be surprised at anything Tootz might say," Jake reminded them as Helene parked the car before a tall, expensive apartment building on the Drive. "Tootz, otherwise Henry Gibson Gifford."

"I remember him," Helene said. "He had a house in Maple Park, and stables. Didn't he lose everything but his shirt in the market?"

"Everything but his horses," Jake said. "The shirt went too, but he still has the horses."

Helene scowled, puzzled. "I thought the stables burned, horses and all, just about the time of the crash."

"Right," Jake said, "but he still has the horses." And as she stared blankly at him, he grinned. "Be patient, pet. You're going to meet Tootz' horses. You're going to meet them any minute now!"

CHAPTER 8

The immense room, overlooking the lake, had satiny paneled walls, a massive fireplace, polished and graceful furniture. At a small table between two long windows, a couple sat playing chess.

The man was slender, dignified, scholarly. His carefully brushed hair and trim mustache were snowy white, his handsome profile was pale and patrician. The hand that paused over the chessboard was long and graceful and pallid. The cut of his dinner coat was irreproachable.

The girl might have been either his daughter or his granddaughter. She wore a simple white frock, almost childlike in its cut and design, with a little string of coral beads at her throat. Her heavy, dull-gold hair curled about her shoulders; her cheeks were pink, dewy, exquisite.

There was nothing in either her appearance or manner to indicate that she had discovered the murdered body of her ex-lover the night before.

The picture was one that held Jake, Helene, and Malone at the door for a moment. Helene looked at the lovely girl, remembered the passionate intensity of Nelle Brown's voice over the radio, singing some ballad of suffering and despair, remembered the stories Jake had told her of Nelle Brown's life, and decided that either her eyes were lying outrageously or Nelle Brown was a gigantic hoax.

But at that moment Nelle Brown greeted them in the voice that no one in the world could have duplicated. Henry Gibson Gifford rose and welcomed them with the grace and charm of a visiting ambassador.

It was to be, Jake had reminded Helene and Malone in the elevator, purely a social call. Bigges, the butler, brought in cocktails, and Henry Gibson Gifford led a discussion of the situation in Europe, on which he spoke with informed authority. Then he and Helene spoke at length of the Russian ballet, about which both of them seemed to know a great deal, while Jake and Nelle quarreled over a song in the next week's broadcast, and Malone stared moodily out the window. Then Henry Gibson Gifford noticed the little lawyer's apparent boredom, and brought the talk around to celebrated criminal cases of the past decade.

He was, Jake thought, one of the most charming and well-informed men he had ever known.

It was Helene who remarked that the day had been almost perfect as far as the weather was involved. Their host sighed deeply.

"I should have liked to take a walk," he said sadly, "but I didn't think it was safe, even with Nelle."

Helene looked up inquiringly.

"They're beginning to close in on me," Henry Gibson Gifford informed her confidently. "My enemies."

"Oh," Helene said. It was the best she could think of at the moment.

"It's extremely tiresome to be followed all the time," he confided, "especially by such very unpleasant-looking men. But they will do it." He sighed again.

"But usually you feel perfectly safe when Nelle is with you," Jake said.

The man shook his head. "Not today. I have felt a sense of foreboding all day. Very unpleasant. Perhaps it will pass. I hope that it will."

"I'm sure it will," Helene said encouragingly. "I feel the same thing ever so often, and it always passes."

Nelle looked at her gratefully.

"Do you?" Tootz asked hopefully. "And are you ever followed?"

"Often," Helene assured him.

He smiled happily and for a while they talked of Steinbeck, of the situation in China, and of the trends of modern drama.

At last she rose and smiled at Henry Gibson (Tootz) Gifford. "I'm going for a drive with Jake and Miss Brand and Mr. Malone," she announced.

Tootz smiled. "Go ahead."

She went to get a wrap, and they rose to leave.

"I'm glad you don't mind my horses," Tootz said to Helene.

She was startled for only an instant. "Mind them! I adore them!"

He was extremely pleased. "I suspect sometimes Nelle really doesn't think I ought to have them in here. But there isn't any other place for them. And they will come here, no matter what I try to do about it. This really isn't just the place for them. But I don't mind." He paused and said almost defensively, "I *like* horses."

"I do too," Helene said.

"Sometime you must come up and tell me about your horses," he said.

"I will," she promised.

For a few moments they discussed Henry Gibson Gifford's horses in a manner so matter-of-fact that Jake caught himself looking about the room to see if they were really there. Then Nelle said good-by to the white-haired man with such gentleness and affection that Jake felt his throat growing strangely hard, and they went into the elevator.

"Well," Helene almost growled on the way downstairs, "why the hell shouldn't he have horses in his living room if he wants horses in his living room?"

"How long has he been like this?" Malone asked.

"Ever since the—no, not since the night when the stables burned. That was part of it. Everything happened at once. He lost all his dough, and the stable burned with all his horses in it, and he was sick for quite a long time, and I sold the Nelle Brown Revue, and we thought he was well again, and then the horses started coming up to the living room."

"He used to have horse races down on the Drive," Jake added, "and the gang at the studio used to bet on them and then call him up to find out who'd won. He used to get sore as hell about the motor traffic getting in the way. But after he began to be followed by the little dark men, he gave that up. Now he just keeps the horses in his living room. I don't think they get enough exercise myself."

"Tough," Malone murmured laconically.

"Why?" Nelle asked almost angrily. "He's happy. Sure he has a few delusions, but nothing that bothers him, except that he doesn't like being followed. He won't stir out of the apartment unless I'm with him. But he's contented there. He doesn't even mind being left alone in the apartment, not at all. I phone him every little while when he's alone, and he parks right by the phone so he'll hear it ring if I call, and nothing bothers him. The horses are no trouble. He likes horses."

"I mean it's tough on you," Malone said.

"Hell's bells," she said, "I like horses myself."

They got into Helene's long sleek car and began driving south.

Malone, in the back seat, tossed his hat on the floor, lit a fat black cigar, and said, "Nelle, just how did Tootz' delusions begin? I want to know how it all happened."

She stared at him. "Why?"

"Nothing important. I just want to know."

Nelle scowled. "Well. Well, it was like this. We were out at the Maple Park place when it happened. Everything. One day we were rich and the next day we didn't have anything. Tootz took it all terribly hard and terribly quietly, if you know what I mean."

"I do," Malone said, "and go on."

"Then the stables burned. They found out what caused the fire; nobody set it, like the newspapers hinted. It was awful, Malone. All those horses, trapped in there. Tootz wanted to go in and Bigges and a fireman held him, and finally he realized that he couldn't and he just stood there and looked at the stables burning and it was awful, and then Bigges and I took him in the house and he acted like he didn't know what was going on, and Bigges and I brought him down to the apartment so he wouldn't see where the fire had been or smell it, and we got him here and he sort of fainted." She paused and looked at the ceiling.

"Go on," Malone said sternly, "the rest of it."

"Well, I called a doctor, and he said it had just all been too much for Tootz and he needed to be kept quiet for a few days, but he was going to be all right."

"The doctor thought he was going to be all right?"

"Yes. He just needed quiet and some rest. And he left me a prescription for some sedative, and I ran out to the drugstore to get it, and I realized I had twenty dollars in my purse and that was all we had in the world. So the next morning I called up McIvers and I said, 'Do you think you could still sell my show to Goldman?' and he said, 'He'd buy it in a minute, do you really mean it?' and I said I did, so he got hold of Goldman and I went down to the office and signed the contract, and then I realized I'd need someone to look after things for me and I remembered Jake used to manage Dick Dayton so I got hold of him right away." She paused again.

"Boy!" said Jake admiringly, "that's breath control!"

Malone said, "Get back to Tootz."

"Well, the day I signed the contract—" she paused, took a long breath. "I was so pleased because we were going to have a lot of money, and I rushed home and showed Tootz the contract and said, 'Isn't it wonderful,' and he was so pleased. And that very night he said something about ordering oats, and I said, 'For what?' and he said, 'For the horses, these horses,' and sort of waved his hand, and he went on talking and I ran out in the pantry and said, 'Oh Bigges, he's gone crazy, what shall we do?' and Bigges said he'd been afraid something like that might happen, and ever since then Tootz has been like that and Bigges has helped me take care of him."

"And the men following him?" Malone asked.

"That was later. Quite a lot later. It was one day when he'd been for a walk and he came back and said two men had followed him. And we thought it was really true, because he seemed so positive, and after all, a lot of people had lost money when he failed. So I went out with him after that but I never saw anybody, and after a while I realized there wasn't anybody. And since then, he's refused to go out unless I was with him. But Malone, he isn't really crazy.

"I mean, not so he ought to be put somewhere. He's happy, and nobody follows him when I'm with him, and he loves his horses. And except for those two things, he's as sane as anybody."

"Of course he isn't crazy," Helene said gently, "He's just different."

"Oh, Jake," Nelle wailed with sudden anguish. "If Tootz should ever find out anything about this!"

"He won't," Jake assured her. "Malone here is going to fix everything for you."

"Sure," Malone said, "no trouble at all. Part of our regular service."

"Are you really, Malone?" she asked.

"I'm going to find out who murdered Paul March, if that's going to help any," he told her, "and then I'm going to find where your letters are and get them back. Does that make you feel any better?" He spoke with serene confidence.

"It helps," she said. "How are you going to do it?"

"That," the lawyer said, "is the only part I hadn't figured out yet. Where can we get a drink?"

Helene mentioned an address on Oak Street and said, "Who might have wanted to shoot this guy, Nelle?"

"Anybody who knew him," Nelle said, promptly and bitterly.

"Let's narrow the field," Malone said. "What do you know about his private life?"

"Practically nothing except that I used to be in it."

The lawyer grunted in disgust.

"You know," Jake said suddenly, as Helene swerved the heavy car into Oak Street, "it ought to be possible to pick up any amount of dope about him at the place where he lived. Nobody ever had a private life in that place. It's like living in a zoo."

"We could question all the people in the building," Helene suggested.

"Thus advertising the fact that we knew there had been a murder," Jake said witheringly.

They were silent while Helene performed an almost incredible feat of parking the car.

"Well," she said, "why don't you move in there and just tactfully ask questions?"

"That's no go," Jake said. "Everybody there knows me. They'd suspect something was up."

"Well then, damn it," she said crossly, "I will."

They stared at her.

"Helene," John J. Malone said, "you're colossal."

"I'll move in," she announced, "and get acquainted with everybody in the place—if you don't believe I can do it, watch me—and I'll dig up secrets in Paul March's life he didn't even know he had."

"It might work," Jake said slowly. "Yes, it might work."

Nelle Brown stared at Helene with wide, puzzled eyes. "But Miss Brand. You don't know me from Adam's off ox. Why should you go to all this bother for a person you never saw before?"

Helene looked at her affectionately. "Maybe I like the way you sing and wouldn't like to have you off the air," she said. "Or you might put down that I liked the way you kissed Tootz good-by. Anyway, let's all go in and buy a drink."

CHAPTER 9

About an hour later, Nelle phoned her apartment, learned that Henry Gibson Gifford was tucked in bed and sound asleep for the night.

"Curfew won't ring for hours yet," she reported, coming back to the table. "Let's think of a place where it would be more fun to do our drinking."

Helene thought of half a dozen with no trouble at all. They moved to one of them.

"Mr. Malone, who shot Paul March?" Nelle asked.

"Can't you get your mind off that?" Jake groaned, "And nobody ever calls him *Mr.* Malone."

"Could you get your mind off it?" she asked.

"No," he admitted.

"Tell me how you got to be a radio star," Helene said to change the subject.

Jake groaned again. "That line is out of *last* night's show."

Nelle ignored him. "Well, I was educated in a convent in Quebec, where—"

"Not that one," Jake objected, "the one where you were born on an old planetarium in Louisiana."

"You mean planetation," Nelle said, pronouncing it just like that. "The Quebec story's prettier."

"The other is more fun."

"Well," she began again, "one day when I was singing in the choir in Ottumwa, Iowa,—"

"How does it feel to skyrocket to fame?" Malone interrupted.

"Don't use that phrase; I don't like it," Helene said. "Before you can skyrocket to fame, someone has to set a match to your tail."

For a full five minutes everyone pretended not to know her.

"If I knew where those letters are, I'd feel a lot happier," Nelle said.

Jake sighed. "There she goes again. All right Malone, where are the letters?"

"For that matter," Malone said, loosening his collar and wiping a glistening brow, "where's the corpse?"

"What good is a murder without a corpse?" Helene inquired. "How can you habeas a corpus if you can't find the damned thing?"

"Your legal terminology is a little confused," Malone said severely, "but your intentions are doubtless good."

"She needs a drink to help her think clearly," Jake said, and signaled to the waiter.

Malone leaned on the table and stared at Nelle. "Who knew that March was trying to blackmail you?"

"Nobody but Jake."

"How did March communicate with you?"

"A note," she said. "I got it at rehearsal yesterday afternoon. It was just a few words on a scrap of paper, written in soft pencil and stuck in an envelope. A Western Union boy brought it."

"How much did he ask for?"

"Only five hundred dollars," Nelle said, "but it was too damned much."

"I don't know," Jake said. "Knowing your vivid imagination, I bet those letters are worth a lot more than that."

"What did you do with the note?" Malone asked.

"I stuck it between the pages of my script, then as soon as I could leave rehearsal I took it to the little girl's room, tore it in small pieces, and dropped it down the john."

"It didn't occur to you," Jake said, "you were destroying a piece of evidence that could have sent March to the jug for extortion."

"I thought I was being wonderfully clever," she said sadly.

"I suppose it was in his writing?" Malone asked.

"Oh, yes. And anyway, he signed his name to it, in full. Yours forever, Paul March."

"Did anybody handle your script except yourself?"

"Not until I'd destroyed the note."

"Wait a minute," Jake said foggily. "Nelle. Your script. Remember? It was lost."

Her slender eyebrows formed a pair of question marks.

"Lost," he repeated. "Just before the broadcast. We never did find out what happened to it."

She said very slowly and thoughtfully, "Yes, I remember. But Jake, that was after I'd torn up Paul March's note. I know that."

Jake said, "Hold up everything for a minute and let me think."

There was an anxious silence. Several minutes and two drinks later he looked up, his brows knit.

"He's coming up with something," Helene murmured hopefully.

He ignored her. "Nelle, you said the note was written in pencil. I've been thinking of the kind of paper those scripts are printed on. Do you suppose stuff could come off on them?"

"Out of them maybe," Nelle said crossly, "but not off on them."

"Damn you, this is serious. Isn't it just possible that if you stuck that note between the pages of the script, and the note was written in pencil, enough impression of it came off on the script so that someone holding it up to a mirror could read it?"

"That's a little involved," Malone said reflectively, "but I see what you mean. A kind of transfer process." He paused. "But if that were true, then anybody might have known about the blackmail note — anybody who happened to pick up the script."

"Which means anybody connected with the broadcast," Jake said. "And if that's why the script disappeared, it's a cinch nobody stole it just to get Paul March's autograph."

Malone sighed. "Nothing that leads anywhere," he said. "If somebody killed March to get those letters and blackmail you, there's nothing to do but sit tight until you hear about it. On the other hand, if somebody killed him to get the letters and protect you, you'll also be hearing the news soon."

"If it's the latter, what do I do?"

"Burn up the letters and keep your mouth shut."

"But," Nelle said, turning pale. "Suppose I should be accused of murdering Paul?"

"Don't worry," the lawyer said confidently, "I could get you an acquittal on the first ballot."

"That's not what I'm thinking about," Nelle said anxiously. "It's Tootz. It would be so awful if he knew about this. I don't care about being arrested, I don't even care about the program and my reputation. But Tootz mustn't find out about it, ever, ever, ever. Or Baby. It would be as bad if he found out."

"Why?" Jake asked. "Why Baby?"

Nelle looked at him crossly. "Can't you imagine what Baby might think if he knew I'd had a love affair with Paul, and then was accused of murdering him? Baby is a timid guy anyway."

Jake said, "Hell, I've had enough of this. Let's go to the Colony Club."

The sky was faintly gray when they deposited Malone at the Loop Hotel where he had lived for fifteen years and drove Nelle home. Helene turned north along the drive. Jake felt his eyelids suddenly growing unendurably heavy and closed them for an instant. When he opened them again, the familiar scenes of Maple Park were slipping by the car's windows. He shook and blinked himself awake.

"The only way to enjoy your driving is to sleep through it," he remarked. "But why are we going out here?"

"I want to change my clothes and pack," she told him. "Did you forget I'm moving to Erie Street?"

Jake thought a moment. "Are you sure you want to do this?"

"You couldn't stop me."

It was noon when they walked into the lobby of the Erie Street building. Helene coolly lovely in a crisp white suit, its perfect severity hinting that it cost more than the average man earned in a week.

Molly Coppins, the landlady, an enormous, slightly faded and very amiable blonde, showing only faint signs of a hang-over, was busily sorting papers at the desk. She was delighted to meet Helene Brand.

"Any friend of Mr. Justus is a friend of mine."

"She gets lonely," Jake said. "Don't let her sit around and mope."

"Don't worry," Molly Coppins said, beaming. "Jake, I only have one vacancy that would do for this young lady. Lovely apartment. It's lucky I have it, too—the occupant just moved out yesterday."

She found an enormous bunch of keys, led them through the maze of halls and corners, up a flight of stairs, and down a long corridor. She stopped in front of a door marked 215.

CHAPTER 10

It's one of the nicest apartments in the building," Molly was saying. "Of course, I'll have the curtains washed."

Jake sank down in a worn overstuffed chair and stared dazedly around him. It was a large, square room, with two immense windows that opened onto a fire escape and looked into the back windows of apartments across the alley. There was a slightly battered but still handsome marble fireplace, now stuffed with old newspapers, a tapestry-covered davenport, a day bed in one corner, and a spinet desk in the other. Nowhere was there any sign of the previous occupancy of Paul March. Not so much as an abandoned magazine.

"Didn't Paul March live here once?" Jake asked very casually.

Molly nodded. "Nice young man, too, but a terrible woman chaser. He left rather suddenly."

"Oh, did he?" Jake murmured.

"Didn't even say good-by to me," the landlady went on. "He was away all night, night before last, and in the morning he came and packed a handbag and left without seeing a soul. Sent me a nice note, though, with the back rent and an extra five dollars, asking me to pack his things and send them to him in care of American Express, Honolulu."

"Well, well," Jake said in his most noncommittal voice.

"How do you like it?" Molly asked Helene anxiously, in a tone that suggested renting this apartment to her was the one thing that really mattered in the world.

"It'll do beautifully," Helene said, "I'm crazy about it. I'm moving in right now."

She and Molly settled formalities of rent and receipt. Molly promised clean curtains the very next day, so help her, and left them.

"You don't have to stay here, you know," Jake said, after she had gone.

Helene paid no attention to him. "Jake, Honolulu is a long way from here."

"A very long way," Jake agreed. "By the time the American Express Company gets tired of trying to find Paul March there, and sends all his belongings back, nobody will give a damn about Paul March any more."

"Somebody," she observed thoughtfully, "is being awfully modest about this murder. Help me unpack."

They unpacked a collection of clothes that would have done credit to a Hollywood queen, set a bottle of rye on the kitchen shelf, and stowed away the empty suitcase.

"Tomorrow," Helene said, looking around the room, "I buy vases and stuff at the dimestore, and this will be elegant."

She vanished into the dressing room, reappeared in a pair of lounging pajamas the color of the center of a very pale rose, and opened the bottle of rye.

"I love our little home, dear," Jake said, settling down on the davenport. "Where shall we hang up the goldfish?"

She poured two drinks, set them on a table by the davenport, and sat down beside him.

"What a wonderful way that was to stave off any inquiries about Paul March's disappearance," she said.

"Wonderful, and simple. Anyone who wants to know where Paul March is, if anyone does want to know, will just be told that he's gone to Honolulu."

She sighed. "Jake, where would you hide a corpse, if you had to hide a corpse?"

"It's a problem I've never been faced with, but I'll think about it. Helene, why did you run away from me?"

"Because I was in love with you," she said calmly. "But if you had to hide a corpse, where would you hide it?"

"In the Cook County Morgue," Jake said, "because that's the last place anyone would think of looking for it. Did you really mean that?"

"Of course I mean it. It would be a waste of time though, I think."

"What? Loving me?"

"No. Looking in the Cook County Morgue for Paul March's corpse."

"Damn you," he said, "if you don't stick to one subject I'll get another girl. Do you still love me?"

"Of course I do. It must be hidden somewhere. You can't just make a body disappear into the air."

"Listen," Jake said. "Get the body of Paul March out of your mind for a few minutes, and me into it. Murders are happening every day in the year including holidays, but this may never happen to us again."

"Jake, let's get married."

He dropped the glass of rye he had been holding, it overturned on the carpet.

"Do you mean that?"

"Of course I mean it. But if you're going to go throwing good liquor around that way, I'll change my mind." She found a rag in the kitchen, mopped up the carpet, and poured Jake another drink. "Keep your hands off that until you're sure you won't drop it."

"But Helene," he said stupidly, "we can't."

"Unless you have a wife and five children in Dubuque, we can," she said firmly. "We can and will."

"But you're rich," he said, still more stupidly.

"Good God," she said, "does that make me an old maid for life?"

"It wouldn't be right." He couldn't say it convincingly.

"Jake Justus, are you turning me down?"

"Damn it, Helene, I could never fit into your life."

"I seem to get along all right in yours," she said reflectively. "Jake, are you in love with me?"

He was silent a moment. "Yes, I guess I am. Yes, that's it."

"Well then, if I'm in love with you, and you're in love with me, we'll get married. That's all there is to it."

It did seem like a simple and perfectly plausible idea.

"Well," he said after a while.

"You're weakening," she observed. "Jake, when shall we be married, and where?"

He said very thoughtfully, "We could drive to Crown Point tonight, if we left now."

"Wonderful," she said. "Now you can drink your rye."

The rye helped a little, but he still felt dazed.

"But Helene," he said, in a final struggle. "Helene, your money."

She sighed. "Well, if you're going to be fussy, I can always give it away. I can think of any number of people who could use it. But it would be more fun to keep it. You'd be surprised how much fun we can have with money."

"I have a rough idea," he said, "but—"

"That's all it's good for, to have fun with. You've got to go right on being a press agent because I'll leave you if you ever give it up. I like your being a press agent. I meet so many people that way."

"Well, of course," he began slowly.

"Oh Jake," she said suddenly, "don't make it awful for me to have money. Like being born with a harelip or something. I can't help it. It's just been a damn nuisance all my life, and if it spoils things, I can't stand it. Let's be sensible."

"All right," he said, "we'll be sensible. But I'm going to tell everybody that I'm marrying you for your money. Nobody could ever be able to imagine any other reason."

"If we're going to Crown Point," she said reflectively, "I'd better get dressed, unless you don't mind my being married in pink pajamas."

"It would save time," he told her, "but it does seem a bit expedient."

She looked into his eyes for a long moment. "I can't believe it. I'm really here and you're really here, and we'll never be separated again. It's been so long, Jake."

"The longest year and a half on record."

"I ought to have a new dress," she said after a pause. "But never mind that. I have you, and one can't have everything. After all, Jake, if we're going to be married today, you might kiss me—"

He did, and thought what a very long time a year and a half had been.

"Jake," she said suddenly, and then, "Jake, how do you suppose the body was gotten out of here without—"

Just then there was a thundering knock at the door.

Helene opened the door; it was Molly. "Telephone for Mr. Justus. And Miss Brand, there's a buzzer over your door. Three rings means you're wanted on the telephone."

The telephone was on the first floor. Jake raced down, two steps at a time. It could only be Nelle, or John Joseph Malone. And either one probably meant trouble.

It was Nelle. Her voice was tight and frantic.

"Jake, have you had dinner yet?"

"No, but—"

"Jake, I've got to see you. Meet me at Ricardo's in half an hour. Bring that blonde with you if you can, she's got brains. And Malone, if you can find him."

"But Nelle—"

"I've found out who it was," she said. "The letters. My letters. I know who has them."

Before he could answer, she had hung up.

CHAPTER 11

Never mind," Helene said consolingly. "We can get married tomorrow. And it'll be so nice to find out who the murderer was."

She had dressed in something pale and cool while he was at the telephone. They picked up Malone at his hotel, selected a table in a far corner of Ricardo's, and waited for Nelle.

"I bet Nelle feels relieved at knowing who it is," Jake said, with little conviction.

Malone looked toward the door. "She doesn't look it."

Nelle was coming toward the table, her face stormy.

"The dirty rat," she said as she sat down. "The double-dirty stinking double-crossing bastard ape. I might have known it. Nobody else in the world would think of a lousy trick like that. I always thought he looked like a murderer anyway. And if he thinks for one split second that he can get away with it—"

"Take a drink," Jake said mildly, "and catch your breath."

She took the drink and caught her breath. "I'm not going to do it, that's all. I'm damned and double-damned if I'm going to do it."

"Menu?" said the gentle Italian waiter apologetically.

"Go to hell," she said absent-mindedly.

"You're double-damned if you're going to do what?" Helene asked.

"I might have known all along he'd be the one who had the letters," Nelle said.

"All right," Jake said, "that's a fine dramatic buildup. Who?"

She stared at him. "John St. John, of course."

The waiter took advantage of the momentary silence to come back with the menu.

"Later," Jake said, waving him away, "and bring us a drink."

"And then," Nelle added, "to try to tie me up with a contract like that!"

"Reorganize yourself," Jake said, "and start this over."

"He telephoned and said he had to talk with me and it was urgent. Then he came up to the apartment. Tootz was taking a nap. He said he had the letters."

"He admitted it!" Jake said. "But good God, that's practically an admission of guilt!"

"What of it?" Malone asked. "You're hardly in a position to call a cop."

"He didn't say how he got them except that it was none of my business," Nelle said. "Then he said he didn't want to make any trouble for me. Trouble! The low-down—"

"You can leave your personal impressions of him out of this," Jake said.

She ignored him. "He's nasty," she said, "he's mean. He gives me the creeps. He's got a fancy accent, and he was born in Nebraska. And he's cold-blooded as a fish."

"How do you know?" Jake asked interestedly.

"Pure hearsay," she said indignantly.

"Well, how was I to tell?" Jake said mildly. "After all, there *was* a time when you hadn't sold the program."

Helene said hastily, "But how did he know about the letters and that Paul March was blackmailing you?"

"We'll get to that later," Jake said. "Right now, I want to know what St. John has up his sleeve besides his handkerchief. Go on, Nelle. What's the rest of it?"

"A contract like that," she said indignantly. "It's a conspiracy, that's what it is. And if he thinks he can sell the show to Givvus—you know, Jake, the soap man—he's squirrelly. Givvus and Company!" She produced a lengthy and impolite sound.

"That's very effective," Jake said, "but your narrative is terrible. Try it all over again, possibly from the beginning."

She drew a long breath, took a drink, and lit a cigarette. Jake had the impression that she was mentally counting ten, slowly.

"Start with the contract," he added.

"It's a personal-management contract St. John is having drawn up for me to sign. You know the sort of thing, Jake. Absolute management of all work, all my contracts signed through him, he collects all income and pays me a weekly salary."

"Good God," Jake said.

Nelle said, "That's what I thought."

"But then," Helene said, in a slightly dazed voice, "he could collect all your dough, and pay you fifty dollars a week if he wanted to."

"Hell," Jake said, "he could pay her ten dollars a week. Such things have happened before, but usually because some promising dope signed up with a grafter before knowing any better."

"It's blackmail," Nelle said furiously, "that's what it is."

"And what's this about Givvus and Sons?" Jake asked.

"He's wanted to sell the show to them for a long time," Nelle said. "Givvus is his pet personal account, and with the show sold the way it is, he—St. John—doesn't make any money out of it. If he personally sells the show to Givvus, he'll make a hell of a lot in commissions."

"Well, as far as that part of it is concerned," Malone said, "what the hell do you care?"

"Goldman is such a swell guy," she said, "and things are practically ideal the way they are. He let us run the show, and we let him run his candy business, and there's never any trouble. With St. John running things for the Givvuses, we'd all go nuts. And besides," she added, "it's the principle of the thing."

The waiter appeared with the tray of drinks and waved the menu at them hopefully.

"Go away," Jake said. "Look here, Nelle, he can't do it. Goldman has an option."

She nodded. "But the option is up tomorrow night at six. Goldman and Joe McIvers are such pals that they aren't worried about re-signing the contract. Goldman wanted to do it with a big gesture at the broadcast next Friday and have his picture taken putting his pen to the dotted line. St. John knows that, and he knows that after six o'clock tomorrow night he can sign with Givvus."

"Well," Jake said slowly, "we can get hold of Goldman tomorrow and get the option taken up before expiration, and Givvus can go peddle his soap somewhere else."

"I thought of that," Nelle told him. "But in the first place, Goldman is somewhere up on the Brule River catching fish and Joe is with him, and he isn't coming back until day after tomorrow. And in the second place, the letters."

"What do you mean?" Malone asked.

"The letters St. John has. I don't know how he got them from Paul March, but anyway, he has them and that's enough. He said if I tried to communicate with Goldman or Joe, or didn't do just as he ordered, he'd send half the letters to Tootz and the other half to Papa Goldman himself."

"I can see Papa Goldman," Jake said, musing. "If he once had the faintest idea that you'd ever committed anything worse than dropping a lead nickel in a phone box. Not a pretty picture. Nelle, St. John seems to have you very nicely."

"Give me a little time to think," Malone said. "What does he want you to do?"

"He's planned a secret—very secret—audition for Givvus tomorrow," she said. "Givvus is flying from the East for it. Hardly anybody at the studio knows anything about it and nobody at the agency. Rehearsal at eleven and the audition in the afternoon."

"If Givvus is all set to sign the show," Jake said, "why the hell does he have to have an audition? Hasn't he heard it on the air?"

"He wants to hear it the way it would be presented for his product, I suppose," Nelle said. "That's all I know. Ask St. John."

Jake said, "I'm God damned if I'll ask St. John anything, even the time of day. Malone, what are we going to do?"

"I don't know yet," Malone said, "unless we could pin the Paul March murder on St. John in such a way that Nelle would be protected, and do it between now and tomorrow night, when the option on your show expires."

"Easy," Jake snorted, "especially as we don't know where the body is, and anyway maybe St. John had nothing to do with it."

"He must have done it," Nelle said, "he's a murdering bastard if there ever was one."

Malone said, "Let me think."

"Go ahead and think," Helene said. "We'll watch."

The waiter appeared out of nowhere. "Perhaps now," he began.

"Look here," Jake said sternly, "the minute we're ready to order, we'll send you a telegram."

"You're breaking his heart," Helene said sympathetically.

"Listen," Nelle said suddenly, "could we bluff him?"

"Possibly," Jake told her, "but it's my hunch he'd just keep on coming back with that menu until we gave in and ordered."

Nelle's retort was brief, appropriate, and highly colored.

"Couldn't we tell St. John we'd found Paul's body," she said more calmly, "and that we knew he'd killed him, and that if he didn't give back the letters and forget this audition, we'd tell the police?"

"Wonderful," Jake said. "Can't you see how the police would love it? What murder? Where's the body? Who did it? Prove it. Where's Paul March? Gone to Honolulu along with his luggage. And even if we could prove there had been a murder, St. John knows that to try to prove it would drag the whole story into the open, letters and all."

"Well," she said unhappily, "it was the best I could think of. How are you doing, Malone?"

"It seems to me," Malone said, mopping his face, "the best thing for you to do is play along with him. Go ahead and put on the audition and somehow delay the signing of the contract just as long as you can."

"What good will that do?" she asked.

"If Goldman signs the contract first anyway, St. John will be up a tree very nicely. With the contract signed with Goldman, St. John can't turn up the letters without destroying a valuable property for his agency, which would put him in the soup. His one chance is to get his contract signed first, just as quick as the Goldman option expires."

"That's right," Jake said.

"So," Malone went on, "you play along with him tomorrow, and I'll fly up to Brule tomorrow and try to locate Goldman and get his contract signed before St. John can make his move. Apparently you won't have anything to do with the contacting of Goldman, and St. John's stunt will just fall through."

"And the letters?" Nelle said.

"I said, he won't be able to use them without destroying a valuable property for his agency. There's only one thing he'll be able to use his letters and his damned personal-management contract for." Malone described it briefly.

"Malone," Helene said, "you're superlative."

He bowed. "All depending," he said, "on whether I can find this guy tomorrow. I think I can. Anyway, by God, I'll try."

"And I hope," Jake said sternly to Nelle, "this will be a lesson to you."

"It has been," she promised. "I'll never write another letter, even to a vox-pop column. Now where's that waiter? I'm hungry."

They looked around. The waiter was nowhere to be seen.

"Probably gone out to dinner," Helene said.

Malone looked at his watch. "Probably gone home to bed."

Nelle looked apologetic. "I hope you didn't have anything planned for this evening."

"Just to get married, that's all," Jake said crossly.

Malone laughed politely. "That's very funny."

Jake's fingers tightened around the neck of the ginger-ale bottle. "I've had enough. The next person, male or female, who says that to me, gets his face shoved down his neck. And when I say that, I'm not being funny!"

CHAPTER 12

Jake began what he was to remember later as one of the most terrible days of a lifetime by meeting Nelle and Helene for breakfast at Ricketts. The two girls were waiting for him when he arrived, exchanging confidences like lifelong friends.

"Anything happen on Erie Street last night?" he asked Helene, sliding into his chair.

"Not unless you count Molly waking me at three this morning to come downstairs and drink beer," she reported. Adding, "It was terrible beer, but I met a lot of interesting people."

A black-haired waitress came and took their order.

"Eight-thirty is a lousy time for breakfast, if you ask me," Nelle grumbled, "audition or no audition."

"You're showing up at St. John's office at ten," Jake reminded her. "You're going to be a nice mild little girl and keep your temper, too. I'll meet you there. First, I've got to deliver a copy of your contract to Malone, so he can fly up to Brule with it."

Nelle said, "I hope to heaven he finds those guys."

"He will," Jake said confidently. "When Malone starts out to do something, he does it. St. John will probably get *his* contract signed, sealed, and delivered at one second after six, official Western Union time. But in the meantime Malone will have the other contract signed before six. St. John's contract won't be worth the match to set it afire." He hoped it was true.

"Isn't he wonderful!" Nelle said. "If it weren't for Tootz, I'd cut you out, Helene, and marry him myself."

"You couldn't do it," Jake said. "It's bad enough to be your manager."

She frowned. "But Jake. Even if St. John doesn't get away with selling me to Givvus, suppose he still makes me sign the personal-management contract?"

"He can't do it," Jake said. "He's got your letters, sure. He can hold them over you, sure. But he can't do more than bluff. Because he knows that to use them would ruin you as a radio property, and after all, no matter who you're sold to, you're his agency's property. Your show is the backbone of the whole damn radio department, of which he's the head. No, he can't use those letters and he knows it."

"I hope you're right."

"I know damned well I'm right. You go through this audition today like a good girl and behave yourself. And then when this is settled, maybe Helene and I can find time to get married."

"Maybe," Helene said gloomily.

"I'll give you a special wedding present to make up for all this," Nelle said. "I don't know what yet, but something."

"How about the Michigan Avenue Bridge?" Jake suggested.

He managed to keep them from talking about the audition until breakfast was over. As he called for the check, Helene lit a cigarette, looked reflectively at the litter of cigarette stubs, matches, and crumpled cigarette packages in the ash tray, and laid her lighted match in the center of it. A sudden blaze leaped up. The black-haired waitress came running.

"Don't mind her," Jake said, in a whisper that could be heard clearly across the street. "She's a pyromaniac. A firebug. She's all right every other way, but she's a pyromaniac."

"Yes," Nelle added in an equally stentorian whisper, "we have to watch her every minute."

Helene busied herself with her compact and pretended not to hear.

"Only last month," Jake finished, "she burned down the railway station in Oshkosh, and it cost us a fortune to hush things up."

As they waited for the change, they could see the black-haired waitress talking in low tones to the other waitresses, who stared with scandalized and fascinated eyes at Helene.

"See," Jake said, "now you're famous. That's what having a press agent means."

Helene closed her compact with a snap. "You're going to be sorry for this," she prophesied gloomily.

A few minutes after ten, Jake walked into the ornate reception room of the agency. Malone was on his way north with the contract. Helene was to meet him at the studio later in the morning.

"Is Mr. St. John in?"

The pretty girl at the desk looked up. "Oh Mr. Justus. Thank God. You'd better go right in."

Jake went down a long corridor, stopped before a desk where a blonde secretary busied herself with pages of reports.

"'Morning, dear. How does your boss feel this morning?"

The blonde girl looked up grimly. "He was peevish when he came in. It's his bunions again. They're always worse on hot days like this. I tell him it's the shoes he wears, but he can't seem to find any that help, poor man. And then Miss Brown came in. She doesn't seem to feel so good either. You'd better go on in."

Through the glass door he could hear Nelle's voice raised to shrieking pitch.

"No," he said, shaking his head, "no, she doesn't seem to feel so good."

He opened the glass door just in time to have a script, thrown from across the room, catch him full in the face.

"Pick that up, Nelle," St. John said coldly.

Jake closed the door. "Is everybody happy?"

"Jake, tell him to go to hell."

"Go to hell," Jake said agreeably, reaching for his cigarettes.

"I asked you to pick up the script, Nelle," St. John said.

Jake started to reach for the script, but Nelle was ahead of him. She picked it up, tore it very slowly and deliberately into shreds, dropped the shreds on the floor, and ground them under her slender heels. Then without a word she stalked out, slamming the door with a bang that set all the windows rattling.

"Nelle don't like the script, eh?" Jake said, lighting a cigarette.

"That's my impression," St. John said crisply. He scowled. "She ought to be made to come back and close that door properly." Jake wondered if St. John had ever taught school.

"It's none of my business," Jake said easily. "Fight the script out between you. But if you want to get a good job from her this afternoon, go a little easy. Nelle has to be pampered a little."

"She's had too much pampering," St. John said nastily. "That's the whole trouble with her."

Jake sat down on a corner of the big desk, swung one long leg back and forth, and said very casually, "It's still none of my business, but why don't you leave Nelle's show with Goldman, who won't buy anything else, sell some other show to Givvus, and have two big shows on the air instead of one?"

"Givvus also won't buy anything else," the agency man said.

Jake looked very intently at his left shoe. "In that case, why go to all the bother of holding an audition for him?"

"Purely a formality," St. John said.

Jake nodded. "Well, I said it was none of my business. A job is a job to me. Let me know what you want Nelle to do, and I'll see that she does it." He looked up at the pale, narrow face across the desk and thought what fun it would be to muss it up.

"I appreciate your co-operation," St. John said. "Let's go on to the studio. I trust Nelle will be there when we arrive."

"She will be," Jake said, hoping it was the truth.

St. John called the blonde secretary, gave orders regarding a dozen or more small details of the day's activities, reached for his shoes under the desk, and put them on with a wince. For the barest moment Jake saw him as a tired, exasperated man whose feet hurt.

They rode to the studio in silence.

Nelle was there, so was Helene. St. John looked at the latter disapprovingly.

"This is supposed to be a secret audition."

"Miss Brand is my confidential secretary," Jake told him. He went on into the control room. Schultz was there, gloomily gnawing an apple.

"What's this secret audition about?"

"Don't ask me," Jake said. "Agency doing."

Schultz grunted.

Oscar Jepps' enormous bulk suddenly darkened the room. "Who the hell wrote this script?"

"Don't ask me," Jake said easily. "Maybe St. John wrote it himself."

Oscar snorted. "I don't think anybody wrote it. I think it was found floating up the Chicago River in a beer bottle."

He rounded up his cast and went into the studio. Helene came into the control room and sat down by Jake's side. Rehearsal got under way.

It was worse than any rehearsal Jake could remember, and that, he reflected, was saying a great deal. There was no single line of the script that met Oscar Jepps' approval. Lou Silver had had to break a date with a new girl friend to attend the audition, and he hated everybody. There was an obbligato passage in Nelle's first song which she foozled on every attempt. The sound-effect man's wife was in the process of having a baby, and whenever a sound cue appeared in the script, it developed that the prospective father had gone to phone the hospital. Bob Bruce had a bad hangover.

During the first half-hour, Nelle burst into tears and walked out of the studio. Through the loud-speaker, Jake could hear Oscar saying anxiously, "Don't worry, she'll sing it all right when the time comes."

During the second half-hour, Bob Bruce went through a brief period of being unable to pronounce "broadcasting" any other way than "croadbasting," and demoralized the entire cast.

After a horrible hour, a timing rehearsal was called, and it was found that the show ran six and three-quarter minutes overtime.

St. John and Oscar retired for a profane and vituperative session of shortening the script, and Jake sent downstairs for coffee and sandwiches for the cast. He looked for Nelle, found her distractedly pacing the hall. Helene slipped an arm around the singer's shoulders.

"I suppose I'll live through this," Nelle said unhappily.

They strolled into the reception room. Someone had left an early *American* lying on one of the chairs. Jake picked it up, glanced at it.

Two Hurt in Plane Crash

"Oh God," Jake said. "It couldn't be!"

Chicago Lawyer Slightly Hurt
in Crash Near Madison

John J. Malone, prominent Chicago attorney, was cut and bruised in the crash of a private plane near Madison, Wisconsin, early today. The pilot is reported in a serious condition. The accident occurred when . . .

CHAPTER 13

Pull yourself together," Jake said. "He still may be able to make it." He hoped his voice carried the conviction that he didn't feel.

"But if he doesn't," Nelle said desperately, "if he doesn't—" She paused, frowned. "I could do this. I could do such a lousy job of the audition that Givvus wouldn't buy the show for marbles."

"You could," Jake said, "but it probably wouldn't do any good."

"Givvus might insist on another audition, which would mean we had a little more time."

"I doubt it like hell," Jake said. "He's heard you on the air. St. John said the audition was a mere formality. And anyway, baby, I don't think you could do it. I hate like the devil to compliment you, but I don't think you could do that bad a show."

She smiled at him wanly.

"Don't worry," Helene said vaguely and helpfully.

Oscar appeared in the reception room, his round moonface shining with sweat. "Script's ready." He wiped his brow. "This is awful."

"At least there haven't been any fights in rehearsal," Jake said consolingly.

Oscar nodded. "That's what worries me. They aren't really putting their hearts into it."

Jake started to follow him to the studio. A page boy touched his arm.

"A lady to see you, Mr. Justus."

Essie St. John was waiting by the elevator, her homely face pale with anxiety.

"Jake, where can we talk? I mustn't be seen here."

He opened a door leading out of the reception room, led her into the seclusion of the stairway.

"Jake, I had to warn you."

"Of what?" Jake said stupidly.

"I don't know what. That's the trouble. You must think I'm nuts. But John's up to something. I can tell. That nasty, pleased way he acts when he's up to something."

Jake nodded. "It's all right, Essie. I know all about it. He is up to something, but he isn't going to get away with it."

Her cape slipped aside and as she moved to retrieve it, Jake caught the outline of an ugly bruise on her shoulder.

"Essie, why don't you leave him?"

"I would if I could," she said dully. "Jake, he's told me again and again that if I do, he'll divorce me, and bring all sorts of horrible things out in court. He can do it, too." She patted aimlessly at her hair. "I couldn't help going out and having a little fun once in a while. You don't blame me, do you? But he knows all about it, and I don't dare leave him."

Jake patted her arm a little awkwardly.

"Someday I'll decide to shoot him," she said in a tired voice.

"I'll buy you the gun," Jake promised.

She smiled weakly. "I've got to know how things turn out today. But I don't dare let him know I'm here."

"Wait in the little girl's room," Jake said. "I'll send Nelle in to tell you about it, when it's all over."

He gave her elbow a reassuring squeeze and walked back to the control room.

Rehearsal dragged on dispiritedly. Oscar Jepps went through all his tricks: was by turns insulting, cajoling, enraged, unhappy. None of them did any good. It was midafternoon when he looked up at the clock and announced, "Dress rehearsal."

Dress rehearsal was not quite so bad as Jake had expected, though Nelle went to pieces on the obbligato passage.

In the interval that followed, St. John slipped away to usher Mr. Givvus into the sanctity of a client's room down the hall, where he would listen to the audition in peace, privacy, and a restful atmosphere. The sound man went to phone the hospital. Schultz went out to buy a chocolate bar. Lou Silver went to make a date with the studio hostess. Bob Bruce went to put cold water on his forehead. Nelle came into the control room, sat down at the black-and-chromium desk, and laid her head on her arms.

"Jake, I'll have to do a deliberately bad job. It's the only way."

He laid a hand on her shoulder.

"And it kills me to do it, Jake. You'd understand why. But the rest of the gang wouldn't. Oscar and Lou and Bob, and even Schultz. They'd always remember I'd done a lousy job of an audition."

"Maybe they'd understand too," he said.

"Well damn it," she said, "I'd always remember it. Even with things as they are. I've never done a show badly in my life."

"That's just pride," he told her.

"All right, damn it, it's just pride."

She rose wearily and paced the little control room while Oscar shooed the musicians and audition cast into the studio, located Schultz and the sound man, and began explaining a last-minute change in the script to Bob Bruce, who didn't look as though he understood it. Schultz put a bag of almonds on the desk and sat down by the control board. Finally St. John arrived, limping ever so slightly.

"Why aren't you with your client?" Nelle asked irritably, picking up her script.

"He wants to listen to this alone," St. John said, "and besides, I don't entirely trust you. I want to be here where I can keep an eye on you." He looked at her coldly. "Too bad you haven't a trained voice. You might be able to come within a few feet of hitting that obbligato."

Nelle started to speak, closed her mouth grimly, reached up with a sudden motion, grabbed St. John's long thin nose between her fingers, and pulled it until he forgot his dignity and yelped. Then she walked stiffly into the studio.

It was, Jake thought, the only happy moment of the day.

St. John retired to a chair in the corner. No one dared look at him.

"All set," Schultz called into the communicating microphone. He looked at his signals and saw that the client's room was ready.

They were not all set. The sound man was missing again.

Someone located him. Oscar looked over the studio and saw that every-one was present.

"Everybody ready?" he called.

"No," Lou Silver said.

The tuba player had the hiccups.

At last Schultz gave the signal, Bob Bruce gave another signal, there was a long sweeping chord on the harp, and Nelle's voice came floating into the control room.

Exactly three minutes later, Schultz jumped, gave another signal that silenced everyone in the studio, and grabbed the communicating micro-phone.

"Start over. I forgot to pipe you into the client's room."

Oscar's groan came through the loud-speaker like a blast from a river boat. St. John said crossly, "Why don't you know your business, Schultz?"

Schultz jumped up. "All right, damn you, you can get another opera-tor." He started for the door.

Jake grabbed his arm. "Sit down, Schultz. For the love of God, let's get this over with."

Schultz hesitated, grumbled, sat down, made motions with plugs and switches. The signals were made again. The long sweep of the harp strings was repeated. Once more Nelle's voice filled the control room.

The audition was finally under way.

Jake thought he had never seen Nelle quite so pale. And no wonder. A lovely spot to be in, he reflected, simply lovely. With the fierce pride of the artist, to do a deliberately bad job would be a thing she'd remember forever. To do a good job would be to cut her own throat.

He listened anxiously till she approached the obbligato passage in her first song. She came to it, her voice picked it up and carried the notes superbly, perfectly, triumphantly. That was the moment when the rest of the cast caught her spirit, and the show began to move.

As the last notes of the closing theme died away, Jake decided that the audition had been as close to perfect as any show Nelle had ever done.

Malone had certainly better find Goldman now!

He walked into the studio, Helene at his side, and saw that Nelle knew how good a job she had done. She was very white, and her eyes were tired. He took her arm firmly.

"Jake—"

"Yes, I know. Nelle, we've got to stall somehow. Helene, you go phone

Nelle's apartment, tell the butler to phone here in about ten minutes with the news that Tootz has had a stroke. We'll have to rush Nelle to his bedside."

"But at six o'clock," Nelle began, "at six o'clock, when the option expires —"

"At six o'clock, you'll be shut in a room with Tootz, and a white-clad nurse and a bearded doctor are going to tell St. John that no one can go in under any circumstances."

"Jake, I love you," Helene said.

They walked out of the studio together. St. John met them at the door, his pale face smiling.

"I knew your good judgment would assert itself, Nelle. Now come along and talk things over with Givvus. You too, Justus."

"Sure," Jake said lightly, "why not?"

He told Helene to wait for them in the reception room, squeezed Nelle's hand reassuringly, and followed St. John down the hall.

The agency man paused at the door to the client's room. "No funny business, now."

"Don't worry," Nelle said wearily. "I know when I'm licked."

They opened the door and stepped inside. Mr. Givvus sat, his back to them, before the loud-speaker. He did not rise, not even stir, when they came in.

"Mr. Givvus," St. John began.

Still the man did not move.

Jake walked over to him. Mr. Givvus was slumped a little in his chair. Just behind his right ear was a small, very neat bullethole.

The audition had been wasted on the late Mr. Givvus.

CHAPTER 14

With a quick, instinctive motion, Jake kicked the door shut, and laid one hand over Nelle's mouth before she could scream.

"But he's dead!" St. John said in a curiously flat voice.

"That's not original," Jake said grimly, "but God knows it's true." He took his hand away from Nelle's mouth and pushed her into a chair.

"But," St. John said, "he was alive when I left him here before the audition."

Jake nodded. "Obviously. Unless you shot him yourself."

St. John looked at him wildly. "Why would I shoot him? He was my *client!* I was auditioning for him."

"I don't know," Jake said. Suddenly he looked at the loud-speaker. "St. John, was the loud-speaker turned on when you left him?"

"No. I showed him how to turn it on, and told him when we'd be ready to go ahead."

"Well, it's turned off now. So either whoever shot him turned it off—heaven knows why—or else it was never turned on, which seems more likely to me. And in that case, the murder took place before the audition."

"You mean," Nelle said, and stopped. "You mean we went through all that awful rehearsal and everything and the audition, and then nobody even heard it? You mean the loud-speaker was turned on and the audition came in here, and he was dead all the time?"

"I do," Jake said, "and shut up." He paused for thought.

"If he was shot before the audition, that means practically anybody might have done it. We were all milling around before the audition." He looked closely at Nelle. There was no sign of emotion on her white face.

"But who would?" St. John demanded. "No one here even knew him."

"It was a mistake," Nelle said. "It must have been a mistake."

"Why?" Jake asked.

"Or whoever shot him isn't in the radio business," she said.

"Nelle, what are you talking about?"

"Jake, no one in radio would shoot a prospective sponsor. He must have been mistaken for someone else."

Jake looked closely at the late Mr. Givvus. He had been a small, spare man, with thinning gray hair, and tight, ungenerous lips.

"Look here," Jake said, "we can't stand around here wondering who shot him. We've got to do something."

"Do what?" St. John said in a dazed voice.

"We've got to get him out of here. Think of the hell that would pop if he were found here in the client's room. Everything connected with this unholy mess would come out, including your own shady part in it, St. John. Radio couldn't stand the scandal, neither could you, and especially, neither could Nelle." He was thinking fast. If Nelle had shot him—and who else would have wanted to—the body had to be gotten away as quickly as possible.

"But what can we do?" Nelle demanded wildly.

"Thank God there's no blood on the chair to clean up. He didn't bleed much and it's all on his coat. St. John, you're in this party whether you like it or not. Get"—he thought for a moment—"get Schultz, Oscar, and

Miss Brand. Bring them here. Make it quick, and keep your mouth shut."

"What do you intend to do?" St. John asked, his hand on the door.

Jake said grimly, "I'm going to take Mr. Givvus for a ride."

As the door swung shut, he turned to Nelle.

"Well, you don't need to worry about whether Malone gets to Brule or not."

"Oh Jake," Nelle said, "the poor little guy. Who shot him?"

"I don't know," Jake said. "If you didn't, maybe it was the same guy who shot Paul March, and maybe not. Or maybe Essie shot him thinking he was St. John."

St. John returned. Schultz, Oscar, and Helene were with him. He had explained the situation on the way.

Jake locked the door. "St. John, how many people knew about this audition?"

"Outside of ourselves and the cast—the head of the sales department here. No one else."

"Good. Somehow, we've got to get this guy out of here."

Schultz cleared his throat. "It can be done. There's a back elevator."

"How about the elevator operator?"

"Leave him to me," Schultz said.

"St. John, how did Givvus get here? Car, taxi, what?"

"He told me he walked over from his hotel."

"That helps. You run along and start spreading the information that your client didn't show up for the audition. I'll meet you here later in the reception room. Helene, get your car around to the rear entrance near the back elevator—Schultz will tell you just where. And Nelle, you and Oscar get out in the reception room and start the biggest, noisiest row you can manage. You ought to be able to draw a good crowd. The rest, Schultz, is up to you."

They left to carry out instructions. A few minutes later Schultz returned, carrying one of the smocks worn by the studio musicians and a bottle of whisky. He poured some of the whisky on the smock, put the smock on Mr. Givvus, pulled a beret over his head so that it concealed the bullethole. Mr. Givvus' straw hat bothered him a moment; finally, he stuck it on his own head.

He peered into the corridor. From the reception room they could hear Nelle and Oscar Jepps calling each other names in stentorian tones.

"No one around. Let's go."

They held the dead man upright by draping his arms over their shoulders, and carried him to the waiting freight elevator. The operator sniffed the whisky-laden air disapprovingly.

"Someday one of these horn-tooters is going to get the ax for showing up corned," he observed. "You should of took his smock off, Schultz."

"No time," Schultz said. "Hadda get him out of there before somebody seen him. I'll take the smock off down in the car."

The operator grinned. "That sound man, Krause, is going nuts," he said.

"It's his first baby," Schultz said.

"That ain't it," the elevator man said, "some ape stole his revolver-shot sound effect out of the studio. It's his own invention and he's fit to be tied. He wants to call the police."

"Why the hell would anybody steal a sound effect?" Jake asked.

The elevator man shook his head. "Search me. Probably a gag. Last stop, all out."

They dragged Mr. Givvus to the alley entrance where Helene was waiting with the car. There Schultz took off the smock and beret, and put Mr. Givvus' straw hat over the bullethole. They sat him up in the back seat, propped up with cushions.

"Good luck," Schultz said, and waved at them.

"Where to?" Helene asked, driving down the alley.

Jake didn't answer.

"Well," she said after a few blocks, "only last night I asked you where you'd hide a corpse if you had to hide a corpse."

"Shut up," Jake said, "I'm trying to think."

"And you said you'd never been faced with that problem, and you'd think about it. Well, I hope you've been thinking."

"Drive toward Lincoln Park," Jake said.

The sun had set, and twilight was slowly settling over the city. As they reached the park, the light was shadowy, dim, almost hazy. Jake directed her to a little-frequented drive, and finally told her to stop near a clump of bushes.

There was a park bench on the other side of the bushes, facing the lake. Jake looked around, made certain that no one was in sight, carried the late Mr. Givvus to the park bench, and sat him upright. As a parting touch, he found a folded newspaper in the car, and spread it in the late Mr. Givvus' lap. Then he climbed back in the car.

"Drive on," he said. "You see, when you have a corpse to dispose of, you simply—"

"This time *you* shut up. Where to?"

"Back to the studio," he told her. "I'm going to try to bluff those letters out of St. John."

The reception room was quiet, nearly empty when they arrived. A page boy sat at the desk, absorbed in a copy of *Amazing Stories*. Nelle and John St. John were sitting on one of the davenports in stony silence, as far apart as possible.

Jake smiled at them pleasantly. "Don't ask me," he said amiably. "You'll read all about it in the newspapers. Now St. John, let's have the letters that belong to Nelle."

"I think I'll keep them," St. John said coldly.

Jake had expected that. "You wouldn't like to have me tell the police about your client being shot when and where he was, and about your being the last person to see him alive, would you?"

St. John's lips curved in an unpleasant smile. "And you wouldn't like to have me tell the police how you disposed of the body, would you? I believe it's a criminal offense. And if you did go to the police, I would have to turn the letters over to them as part of the evidence, and of course the newspapers—" He let it go at that.

"Well," Jake said after a pause, "I thought there was no harm in trying."

St. John said, "In view of what has happened, Miss Brown's contract will probably be re-signed with Goldman as expected, so she has nothing to worry about. The letters are in a good, safe place. I think I'll keep them, just in case."

"A general agreement of silence seems to be the most sensible idea," Jake said.

St. John nodded.

"Just the same," Nelle said, crossly, "you might tell us how you got the letters in the first place."

"I got them from Paul March," St. John said.

"Obviously," Jake said, nastily. "What we'd like to know is what you did with his body."

"Body?" St. John repeated blankly. Then he gave a polite little laugh. "Oh yes. That's very funny."

Jake made one sudden and cataclysmic motion. A loud sound shattered the pleasant twilight quietude of the reception room.

"Oh boy!" said Nelle Brown exultantly. "Oh boy! Right on the button!"

CHAPTER 15

A page boy came running and helped St. John to his feet.

"I'm sorry," Jake said. "It was one of those irresistible impulses."

"That's all right, Mr. Justus," said the page boy soothingly. "Those things will happen now and then."

John St. John glared at them over a handkerchief.

"I'm not going to forget this, Jake Justus!"

"Not for a while, you're not," Jake agreed happily, looking at the reddening handkerchief, and the damage done on St. John's slender and aristocratic nose.

"I always say," Helene observed, watching St. John's stiff back disappear through the door, "there's nothing like a good old-fashioned brawl to clear the atmosphere."

Jake flicked imaginary soil from his hands. "Now that's over, we'll have dinner."

"How can you!" Nelle said weakly. "How can you eat or talk or do anything normal, after—after a day like this!"

"We men of iron," Jake said in his best lecture-platform voice, "become accustomed to the trivial frictions of life."

Even this didn't get so much as a snort out of Nelle and Helene.

They had dinner, doing their best to keep up a conversation. It was not wholly successful.

"I wonder if they've found him yet," Helene said over the coffee.

"Found who?"

"The—I mean, Mr. Givvus."

Nelle shuddered. "It was awful. I mean, walking in there and finding somebody murdered."

"You ought to be getting used to it," Jake said. "This is the second time it's happened."

"Jake!"

"We'll take her home," Helene said, "my home, I mean. Then she can feel as bad as she wants to."

Jake paid the check and they walked out to the car.

"We'll take her home," Jake said, "but there's no sense to her feeling bad. Naturally murder is bound to be a little upsetting, but you can get used to anything. And these murders all seem to be doing Nelle a lot of good."

They stopped at the drugstore to replenish the liquor supply, then drove to the Erie Street building.

Halfway up the stairs, Nelle stopped. "Jake. Not that apartment."

"Yes," Jake said, taking her arm. "That apartment. And quit shivering. It doesn't look anything the same."

Helene stopped suddenly. "Oh Lord. I forgot."

"What did you forget?" Jake asked. "I've got the bottle."

"I forgot that—I mean, I forgot it was the same apartment that—"

"Shut up," Jake said, "both of you."

"Oh Jake," Helene said, "can't you sympathize with her?"

"I can," Jake said, "but I'm damned if I think it would be good for her. Go on, open the door." He slipped an arm around Nelle's waist as they walked into the room.

She looked around a little timorously. "It doesn't look the same. Everything's gone. Everything of his, I mean." She began to cry.

Jake steered her to the davenport, sat down beside her, and pulled her head down on his shoulder. "Go ahead. Cry all you want. You might as well get it over with."

"I just thought," she sobbed, "about all the times I used to come here and how everything looked then, and then I didn't come here any more but I knew everything was just the same, and he was here, and now he's dead, and everything of his is gone, and it's all so different."

"Sure," Jake said, patting her. "Go ahead and cry."

"It was just as if I didn't really know what had happened, because so many other things kept on happening, but walking in here like this made me realize everything all of a sudden, Jake, and it's awful."

"A lot of things are awful," Jake said, "but you get used to them."

"I won't ever get used to this, Jake. I'll just keep thinking about walking in here and finding him dead, even when I'm an old woman and all my teeth fall out and nobody likes me any more, and I'll never forget any of it, Jake, and I'll never be happy again as long as I live, never, never, never."

"Cheer up," Jake said, "you haven't got hay fever."

She stopped crying and looked at him. "What about hay fever?"

"I mean," Jake said, "think how terrible it would be if all this happened to you, and you had all these troubles, and then on top of everything else, you had hay fever. That would really be awful."

She was silent for a minute, finally managed a smile.

"Maybe I ought to have a drink."

"Maybe you ought to wash your face first," Jake said.

She thought about it. "I guess I will."

Jake strolled out to the kitchen where Helene was busy with glasses and the bottle of rye. "I'm glad that's over."

"I don't know but what I do approve your variety of sympathy after all," Helene observed. "Maybe it was a good idea to bring her here. She's going to feel a lot better from now on." She carried glasses and the bottle into the living room, poured drinks and set them on the table, and sat down on the floor.

Nelle returned, her face duly washed.

"Well," Jake said, putting a glass in Nelle's hand, "now perhaps we can try to dope this thing out."

"Jake," Nelle asked, "who shot Mr. Givvus?"

"Did you?" he asked, very calmly and quietly.

She stared at him. "Jake, you really think that I did?"

He avoided her eyes. "Well after all—you were there. You had the best reason for it, as far as I know."

"Jake, don't be a fool," Helene said furiously. "You know she didn't shoot him."

He sighed. "I don't *know* anything. She might have, and could have. That's why I was so ding-danged anxious to get the body away from there."

"But I didn't, Jake," Nelle said, desperation in her voice.

"All right, we'll go on the assumption that you didn't, and God help you if you're lying about it. If you didn't—who would want to shoot Mr. Givvus?"

"A question," Helene said. "Who at the audition would know him well enough to want to shoot him?"

"As far as I know," Jake said thoughtfully, "the only person there who knew him was St. John. How about it, Nelle?"

"You're probably right. I met him once, months ago. He's from Philadelphia. I don't imagine one solitary soul at the broadcasting studio knew him, except perhaps for a casual introduction. What's more, it being a secret audition, nobody outside the cast and ourselves knew he was there—and I'm sure nobody in the cast knew him."

Jake sighed. "That leaves us you and St. John," he said. "And God knows, St. John wouldn't have shot him. Not after arranging a secret audition of a show to sell him and going through all a secret audition means—and on a day when his bunions hurt, too. No, even if St. John had wanted to shoot him, he'd have let him hear the audition first."

"And that leaves me," Nelle said slowly. "But Jake, I didn't."

"All right," Jake said, "let it go at that. There's one very pertinent fact that you yourself innocently pointed out when we found the body. Remember? You said—'But nobody would shoot a prospective sponsor. He must have been mistaken for someone else.' "

"He was sitting with his back to the door," Nelle said slowly, "with just the back of his head showing. And the lights weren't any too bright in the client's room. They're kept dim on purpose, so that prospective sponsors won't start reading timetables when they're supposed to be listening to auditions. But who could he have been mistaken for?"

"Who else would be in the client's room during the audition?"

"Nobody but St. John." She paused, and stared at him. "But Jake, that means somebody wants to murder St. John. And we've been thinking all along that St. John was the man who shot Paul March!"

"Maybe he did," Jake said. "That doesn't mean he's the only potential murderer in town. This afternoon's mistake, assuming that it was a mistake and the shot was meant for St. John, may be an entirely different affair."

"Who would have wanted to murder St. John?" Helene asked.

"Anyone who knew him," Nelle said promptly and nastily.

"That's what you said about Paul March. Not much help," Jake said. He sighed. "The client's room is down the hall from the studio and away from the reception room. Which means that before the audition, anybody connected with the show might have gone in and shot him. Or anybody else might have, during the audition, including Essie St. John, who was around waiting for news about the audition. I hope she isn't waiting there yet."

Nelle said, "Do you think she shot Mr. Givvus, thinking he was St. John?"

"If she did," Jake said, "I think she's entitled to another try." He thought a minute. "It's funny nobody heard the shot. It's funny nobody heard the shot when Paul March was killed. Maybe someone is using a gun with a silencer. But that would indicate the same person was responsible, and there isn't any connection between the two murders except Nelle."

"Jake," she said earnestly, "Jake, I didn't."

"You've said that before too," he told her.

The sudden sound of the buzzer over the door made them all jump. Jake went to the door, found the call was for him, and went down to the telephone, noticing on the way that another noisy party was getting a good start in the room next door. Almost as noisy as the last one had been.

The call was from Malone, still in Madison.

"Never mind," Jake told him, "everything's fixed. I can't explain it over the phone, but you don't need to find Goldman now. And for the love of Pete, get back here as quick as you can. We need you!"

"For what?"

"To be best man at a wedding," Jake said, and hung up.

He started up the stairs, wondering how long it would take to drive to Crown Point in the morning. As he reached the top a sudden, loud noise came through the closed door of apartment 215.

The door of the room housing the noisy party burst open and the hall was full of people. A disheveled brunette caught at Jake's arm.

"That noise! What was it! Where did it come from?"

"It came from in there," Jake said grimly, racing toward the door, "and it was a revolver shot!"

CHAPTER 16

Jake's mind was spinning like a top as he raced down the hall. The gun. Who had fired it? Nelle? Was she the murderess after all, and had she— Oh no, not Helene. It couldn't be. Or had someone come in while he was at the telephone, and—

He flung open the door, the disheveled brunette at his heels, the others close behind.

Nelle sat on the davenport, calmly smoking. Helene stood in the middle of the room, a peculiar contraption of wood, rubber, and leather in her hand.

"Good God!" he said, and again, "good God!"

"What happened?" the brunette cried.

"The gun," Jake said, "where—"

"I've got it," Helene said. She suddenly released a spring on the peculiar contraption. The room resounded with the sound of a gunshot. The brunette screamed.

"Holy Moses!" Jake said. "It's Krause's sound effect!"

Helene laughed. "I'm sorry I frightened anybody."

For the first time Jake was aware of the little crowd in the doorway.

"You certainly frightened us all right," said a thin young man with a dark mustache. "You certainly frightened us!" He mopped his brow.

Helene looked surprised. "You mean you could hear this thing all the way down the hall to your room?"

"Hear it!" the young man said, "I thought the little men were landing from Mars!" He mopped his brow again. "I'm glad no one was shot. Come on down and have some beer."

Helene brightened. "We'd love to," she said. "But to make up for frightening you, let me bring along a drink. Besides, I just moved here, and I ought to buy the drinks." She tucked the bottle under his arm and they followed her through the door. Jake waved to Nelle to come along.

No one bothered with such trivialities as introductions.

"A whole quart!" the young man said admiringly. "You're going to be a wonderful addition to the neighborhood!"

The young man's room was small, and there were only two chairs and a bed to sit on, but no one minded. After the rye was gone, Jake went to the corner for two half-gallon bottles of beer, and then the young man with the mustache went to the corner for two more half gallons. Then someone else went to the corner for more rye. By that time Jake had learned that the previous occupant of Helene's apartment had been named Paul March, that he had been a very handsome young man who had something to do with the radio business, that he'd owed a little money to nearly everybody in the building, that he'd promised the disheveled brunette to get her a job on the radio, and that he'd once had a blondish girl friend, described as pretty by the mustached young man.

Except for the beer, Jake had a feeling that the evening had been wasted.

At last he rounded up Nelle and Helene and they left, after a slight argument with someone who wanted to know how Jake could get away with taking two women home from the party. The three of them went into Helene's apartment and shut the door.

The sound effect still lay on the table. Helene picked it up and looked at it thoughtfully.

"Don't do it," Jake begged. "This time someone will call a cop."

She sighed, and put it down.

"Krause will have you arrested," he observed. "He loves those things like a mother. What did you do it for?"

"I wanted to know if you could hear a revolver shot down in that room when a party was going on, and I found out. You could."

"Yes," he agreed, "you certainly could."

"So why didn't they all come down to find out what had happened the night Paul March was shot?"

"Oh," Nelle said, "I see now!" She paused. "It's a pity you can't go and try that in the client's room where Mr. Givvus was shot, and see if it can be heard in the reception room—"

"Don't suggest it," Jake said with feeling. "You don't know her. She'll try it."

Helene sniffed. "I don't need to try it. I'm sure nobody heard the shot this afternoon, or it would have been investigated. Therefore, no one did."

"Therefore," Jake picked it up, "someone used a gun with a silencer in both cases, and that must mean the same person committed both murders. I'll believe just so far in coincidence, and no farther. Helene, when are we going to get married?"

"Tomorrow," she said promptly. "But Jake, it was St. John who shot Paul March. It must have been. And that means—"

"Can you imagine St. John shooting a prospective client during or before an audition?" Jake asked scornfully. He looked searchingly at Nelle. "Nelle, if by any chance you're lying to me about this, I'll break your neck, so help me God."

"But I'm not lying to you," she said desperately.

He sighed. "As a matter of manners, I'll believe you. But you could have done both murders, and you had a motive for each of them. In the second one you had a motive that worked both ways—I mean, whether you thought you were shooting St. John, or knew you were shooting Givvus, your contract would be all right."

"Do you think I'd commit a murder for a *contract?*"

"Hell," Jake said, "for a good contract you'd do much worse than that."

"Stop picking on her," Helene said indignantly.

"Don't mind me," Jake said mildly, "I'm just trying to solve a couple of murders."

Helene frowned. "Find someone who had a motive for murdering both Paul March and either St. John or Mr. Givvus."

"And then," Jake said, "find who had the opportunity in both cases, and has a gun with a silencer on it, and then pin it on this unknown person in such a way that Nelle won't be dragged into it, and then get her letters back safely." Jake sighed. "Nelle, this woman hasn't any more liquor. Let's go home."

Nelle rose to her feet a little uncertainly. "I've got to go home anyway. It's late."

"I'll drive you home," Helene said. "You too, Jake."

In the first-floor hall they ran into Molly, looking very forlorn and on the verge of tears.

"Thank God!" she exclaimed. "If I hadn't found anyone to have a drink with me, I'd have gone right out the window."

They paused long enough to help her finish a bottle of gin, and listened while she told them about her life, which had been unquestionably very sad. Then Helene performed a miraculous feat of driving that landed them in front of Nelle's apartment building, and Jake saw her safely into the elevator.

"I'll send the sound effect back tomorrow, anonymously," Helene said on the way back, "if it's on your conscience."

"It's not on my conscience," Jake said, "but with a new baby and a wife in the hospital, Krause has enough trouble without losing his revolver-shot sound effect. Helene, you don't want to go home. I don't want to go home. It's still early. Only two o'clock. We're still sober. Let's go somewhere and buy a drink."

"We'll do nothing of the kind," she said firmly. "I'm taking you to your door, and you're going right upstairs and go to bed and go to sleep. Then I'm putting the car away and going home myself. You may have forgotten it, but you're going to be married tomorrow."

Jake sighed deeply. "I'm afraid that matrimony is going to be a terribly sobering influence on you," he said thoughtfully. "Maybe I won't marry you after all."

She drove in silence for half a block.

"All right," she said, "all right. But we only stop for one drink. One!"

CHAPTER 17

Jake woke from a dream that was half hang-over and half night-mare, wondered if his eyes felt more uncomfortable open or shut. He thought very seriously for a little while, and then resolved that this would be the beginning of a new and far, far better life.

There was a dim—but very dim—recollection of taking Helene home in a taxi. He wondered where they had left her car, and if they would ever find it again.

He remembered that there was something about today that was terribly important. Or had that been part of the dream he had just left behind him? No, he was sure—quite sure, anyway—that it was something real. Not a delucination. Delucination? What was that? Oh yes, it was what Tootz had. A cross between a delusion and a hallucination.

He wished he hadn't waked up.

What was it that was so important? Something that made today different from all the other days in history, his history or the world's. Something that he was going to do.

He wished he could remember what it was.

He was still trying to fix his mind on it when the telephone rang. It was Helene.

"Today we're getting married, or had you forgotten?"

"I was just trying to work it into the schedule," he said gallantly.

"I thought maybe you'd just remembered you already had a wife in St. Louis."

"It isn't St. Louis, it's Allentown," Jake said in a surprised voice, "but how did you know?"

"Maybe I'm just discouraged, but I have a feeling we'll never get to Crown Point."

"There's no audition today," Jake said, "and no shootings scheduled as far as I know. Anyway, nothing is going to interfere this time. Nothing. Do you get that? I'll be over in," he looked at his watch, "half an hour."

He shaved, took a shower, and dressed, spending an extra thirty seconds on the selection of his tie.

Just as he was ready to leave there was a sudden knock on the door. He opened it and there stood Malone, a rakish bandage over one eye.

"The next time I travel, I go on a tricycle," the little lawyer said sourly. He came in and kicked the door shut. "Imagine how I felt when I saw that tree coming at us. Imagine how I felt when I couldn't find any way of getting up to Brule. And imagine how I felt when you told me it had all been a waste of time. Now tell me why I didn't need to find Goldman."

"Somebody shot St. John's client," Jake said, "during the audition. Have you had breakfast?"

"Who shot him?"

"A man with a gun in his hand. Or maybe it was a woman. Have you had breakfast?"

"*No.* What happened?"

"Look here," Jake said, "I've had enough of this. Helene and I are getting married today at Crown Point. I'm on my way to get her now. If you want to come to breakfast, I'll tell you about it on the way. If you don't want to, you can go to hell."

"A very kind invitation," Malone said, "and welcome, too. And if you don't know any better than to get married, it's none of my business. Now tell me about this murder."

By the time they had reached apartment 215, Jake had finished his story of the sudden death of the late Mr. Givvus, and the subsequent disposal of the body. Helene greeted them enthusiastically and invited Malone to go with them as a bridesmaid. Malone agreed but stated his refusal to wear a corsage, and began looking through the morning newspapers, while Jake and Helene quarreled over the process of coffee making and discussed what she might or might not have done with her car the night before.

At last the coffee was made, and Jake spread the newspapers out on the table.

The police were greatly concerned over the discovery of the late Mr. Givvus on a Lincoln Park bench. There were pictures of the bench, and of a policeman named Gadenski pointing to the exact spot where the body had been found. One story mentioned the fact that a copy of a Chicago newspaper had been found in the dead man's lap, turned to a story concerned with downstate vice conditions. Another story gave the same fact, but stated that the newspaper had been turned to a picture of a Hollywood queen. Both stories treated the fact of the folded newspaper as being of extreme importance. But there was no hint of the fact that the late Mr. Givvus had been in Chicago to attend a radio audition.

"Thank God!" Jake said.

Malone scowled, spilling a little coffee on his cuff. "I suppose you know you've committed a serious crime in moving the body."

"Hell," Jake said, "what would you have done? I'm hired to protect Nelle Brown's reputation, one way or another. This was one of the ways. Suppose he'd been discovered in the client's room where he'd gone to listen to a Nelle Brown secret audition?"

"Just the same," the little lawyer said, "they put people in jail just for things like that."

"Well damn it," Jake said furiously, "what have we got a lawyer for? Put your mind on the train of thought that would have followed the discovery of the body. It was a secret audition. Why was a secret audition being held? Papa Goldman comes rushing back from Brule. His Nelle Brown giving a secret audition for another client! Could Nelle explain to him that she had to give the audition because St. John was blackmailing her? Either way, Papa Goldman would have had the best of reasons for refusing to re-sign her contract Friday night."

"Good God," Malone exploded, spilling the rest of the coffee, "two men have been murdered, and all you're worrying about is getting Nelle's contract re-signed."

"All I'm worrying about," Jack said, "is when we're going to get to Crown Point and get married."

"Suppose," Malone said thoughtfully, "suppose someone remembers seeing Givvus going to the broadcasting studio."

"No one did. He wasn't the sort of guy you'd notice. Just a little, ordinary-looking guy."

"Those are the sort of guys that always get noticed," Malone observed. He sat thinking for a minute. "Anyway, if he was a little ordinary-looking guy, it's damned funny somebody mistook him for St. John."

"The light was poor in the client's room," Jake said.

"It couldn't have been that poor."

"The murderer has poor eyesight," Helene suggested helpfully.

"Maybe he has," Malone said, "maybe he has. You've got something there that you probably think is a clue. But we *know* he's a damned good shot." He drew a long breath. "If someone's really trying to murder St. John, there may be a second attempt."

"I hope to God there is!" Jake said crossly.

"All right, but let's get Nelle's letters back from him first."

"Let's get me and Helene married first."

"Let's remember where my car is first," Helene said.

"A fine thing," Jake said indignantly. "I'm only marrying you because I like the car, and here you go and lose it."

"If you could remember where we went last night, maybe I could remember where the car is."

"All this is very interesting," Malone said peevishly, "but don't forget you're mixed up in two murders, you've committed a crime that may land you in the jug, only God knows what's going to happen next, and He in His infinite wisdom refuses to tell." He rose, strolled to the window, and stood looking across the backyard litter of barrels, clotheslines, garbage cans, and tired cats. "I'm following a train of thought."

They were silent for a few minutes.

"It goes like this," Malone said, still looking out the window. "Not *my* train of thought, you understand. But *a* train of thought. It could become very popular, too."

"What the devil are you talking about?" Jake demanded.

The little lawyer didn't seem to hear him. "As Nelle Brown's manager, Jake would find the death of the late Mr. Givvus very much to his advantage. We needn't go too deeply into motives, save that there would be important financial ones. Anything over four bits cash money is an important financial motive these days. There would be friendship motives, too. An unselfish-love motive might hit popular fancy, too." He paused again.

"The late Mr. Givvus," he went on thoughtfully, "was shot at some undetermined time, quite conceivably a time when Jake was on the loose around the corridors of the broadcasting studios. I mention this as another probably popular station at which a train of thought might pause.

"Finally," he said, warming to his climax, "this damned dummox, Jake Justus, goes to work and moves the body, thus concealing the evidence of his crime." He concluded with one magnificent gesture.

After a longish pause he said, mildly, "This, Helene, leads up to the fact that if they hang Jake, you can still marry me."

"But no," she said in a dazed voice.

"Are you turning me down?" Malone inquired pleasantly.

"As I said before," Jake remarked, "what have I got a lawyer for?"

"I'm just a lawyer," Malone told him, "not a miracle man."

"You're a maniac," Helene said angrily. "None of that is going to happen in anyone's mind, and you know it."

Malone shrugged his shoulders. "Suit yourself. The alternative train of thought, which leaves on another track, is that Nelle shot him and Jake moved the body to protect his client and his pal."

"For all I know," Jake said slowly, "that train may be the right one. But damn it, Malone, there's no chance anyone will find out that Givvus was shot at the studios."

Malone said, "A flier will tell you that a good landing is any landing you can walk away from. The same statement applies to good murders. But I have a dirty hunch this murder isn't one you can walk away from."

"What's to be done?" Jake asked.

"I'm gonna see a guy," Malone said. "A police lieutenant by the name of Von Flanagan."

"Come again?" Helene said.

"Von Flanagan," Malone told her, "it's his name. It was Flanagan and everybody kidded him so much about Flanagan being a good name for a cop that he went to court and had the Von tacked on."

"He should have made it Von MacFlanagan," she commented. "Why do you want to see him?"

"I want to remark that I once knew a guy named Givvus and I wondered if this could be the one, which it will turn out it isn't, but meantime I'll find out just how much the police do know about the murder."

"Confessions of a nasty spy," Helene said. "And then?"

"We're going to get married," Jake said stubbornly. "Today."

Malone shook his head. "This first. Before I'll let you two go anywhere, I'm going to make very sure that no one is going to remember Mr. Givvus went to hear an audition yesterday afternoon. Then I'll speed you on your way. I'll even buy the flowers."

"You'll probably pick out a wreath," Jake said gloomily.

Malone found his hat where it had rolled under the davenport, brushed ineffectively at the dust on it, and said, "All I hope is that the day doesn't land you in a police station."

Helene gave a sudden yelp and sprang to her feet. "I've got it! I know!"

"What?" Jake demanded. "What is it!"

They stared at her hopefully.

"My car. I remember now where I left it."

"Oh hell," Jake said. "I thought you know who'd murdered Mr. Givvus. Where is it?"

"I left it by the NO PARKING sign in front of the Chicago Avenue Police Station," she said happily. "I remember thinking at the time, it would be such a good safe place for it!"

CHAPTER 18

Malone knew the desk sergeant at the Chicago Avenue Police Station and managed to convince him of a good reason why the big imported car had been left there overnight between two NO PARKING signs. Then he delivered the car to Helene, suggested to her that his life would be simplified if she took up bicycling, and went in search of Daniel Von Flanagan.

The big police officer was red-faced and wilted by the heat, and very tired. He welcomed Malone's suggestion of a cool drink in some quiet place as a marooned mariner might have welcomed the Coast Guard.

Von Flanagan was a weary, exasperated, and unhappy man. He was, as he explained to Malone, only an honest cop trying to do his duty; and the police department, the D.A.'s office, and the newspapers seemed to hold him personally responsible for the fact that people would murder each other in complicated and devious ways.

"Just a nice straightforward shooting, I can understand," he said dismally into his beer, "but why people should go out of their way to make life so hard for me, I don't know."

"It's probably nothing personal," Malone said.

"Now you take this dame who shot her husband," Von Flanagan went on. "She shot him in the kitchen of their house, there was nobody else in the house, the neighbors called a cop, she had the gun that had killed him, and everybody knew she hated his guts. It was all nice and simple. No fuss, no bother. I arrested her, and you defended her, and she was acquitted, and I understand she's going to marry a guy who owns a chain of taverns on the West Side. Nice fella, too. Now that's the way I like to see things happen. Quick and clean and simple."

"So many people do everything the hard way," Malone said sympathetically.

"Hard for me, you mean," Von Flanagan said. "If I had it to do over again, I'd of been an undertaker like I intended to be in the first place. Believe me, if our alderman's wife's brother hadn't owed my old man

money, I'd of never been a cop. Now you take this guy who was found
shot up in Lincoln Park. He's been driving me nuts all day." He sighed
heavily.

"What about him?" Malone asked. "I didn't read much about it in the
papers, just the headlines."

"More beer," Von Flanagan said to the waiter, "and listen, Gus, you'd
better bring 'em two at a time. A park-district cop named Leo Gadenski
was going along the walk near the viaduct and he seen this guy asleep on
a bench. So he goes to chase him off, only this guy ain't asleep, he's
dead." He sighed again, more noisily. "It's an awful mess."

"Why?" Malone asked disinterestedly.

"Because there ain't no reason for nobody shooting the guy," Von Flanagan exploded. "Nobody wants to shoot him. He comes from Philly, and
he's rich, and he makes soap. That's a hell of a lot to find out about a guy,
now isn't it? I ask you. Nobody knows him in Chicago. Nobody ever
heard of him in Chicago. And God damn it, nobody knows why he came
here." He looked moodily into his glass.

"That don't make sense," Malone said.

"I know damn well it don't make sense. Look here. This guy flew here
from Philly yesterday and got in around noon. We know that. He regis-
tered at the Drake, went up to his room and washed—all he had with him
was a little handbag with a shaving kit and a clean shirt—went downstairs
and had lunch, and walked out the door. We know that. And then what?
Then he turns up in Linoln Park, on a bench, dead."

Malone decided there was a special providence that looked after Jake
Justus. He called for another beer.

"Sounds like he came here on a business trip," he hazarded cautiously.

Von Flanagan nodded. "Yeah, but what business? No one knows anything about it. His company has a sales office here and no one in it even
knew he was in town. He didn't intend to stay long; he had reservations
on the midnight plane." He paused to brush a fly off his cheek. "I've got a
little money tucked away, and next year I'm gonna retire, and do you
know what I'm gonna do? I'm gonna raise mink."

"Mink?" the little lawyer repeated stupidly, his mind still wrestling with
the problem of Mr. Givvus.

"Yeah, mink. Annie's been hounding me for a mink coat for three years,
so last winter I priced one, and do you know what those damn things
cost?"

"I'll tell the world I do," Malone said bitterly and reminiscently. "Can
you learn anything from Philadelphia?"

"Hell no," the police officer said. "Nobody there knew where he was going. He told his office he was going to be away for a day, and that was all. Whatever he came here for, he was sure keeping it dark."

"Maybe somebody followed him here," Malone suggested.

"Do you suppose we didn't think of that?" Von Flanagan said scornfully. "We checked his wife, his kids, his in-laws, his girl friend—boy, was she a handful—his business associates, even his bookie. Nobody followed him to Chicago. Nobody even knew he was coming to Chicago. I tell you, Malone, it don't make sense."

"Well," Malone said, "it's like this. He probably went for a walk in the park and sat down on a bench to rest. Somebody was shooting at birds, or tin cans in the lake, or some damn thing, and plugged him by mistake. Probably don't even know it."

Von Flanagan nodded. "Sure. That's easy. So easy I thought of it myself. Only here's the thing, Malone. He wasn't shot on that park bench. He was took there."

Malone raised an eyebrow, drew a long breath, and said very slowly, "That's funny."

"Funny ain't the word for it."

"How do you know he was taken there?"

"Because," Von Flanagan growled, "when Gadenski found him he'd been dead anyway an hour. Well we found a couple who'd been sitting on that very same park bench not fifteen minutes before Gadenski found the body." He loosened his tie and went on, "Naturally there was all hell popping when the body was found, and this couple was walking along the beach, and they came up to see what all the rumpus was about. And the guy, he says, 'Why, we were sitting on that bench a few minutes ago.' "

"I see," Malone said, nodding, and wondered why Jake Justus's special providence didn't keep its mind on its work.

"So," the police officer finished, "he must have been shot somewhere else, and somebody carted him up to Lincoln Park, and sat him on the bench. Now will you please tell me why the hell anybody would do that?"

"Why indeed," Malone murmured.

"Why not leave him where he was? Or if he had to be carted away for some reason, why sit him up on a bench in Lincoln Park, with his hat on his head, and why the hell stick a newspaper in his lap?" Von Flanagan mopped a steaming brow. "I tell you, Malone, nobody would do a thing like that who wasn't just plain ordinary nuts!"

"You," said Malone soulfully, "are telling me!"

Von Flanagan waved to the waiter for more beer. "See what I mean? It's things like that make life hard for me. Now you take mink. They don't give you no trouble. They're healthy, if you take good care of 'em. And—"

"What are you going to do about the Givvus case?" Malone interrupted.

"I've sure as shooting got to do something. I'm getting hell about it." A grim look came into his mild blue eyes. "And I'm gonna do something, too. I'm an easygoing guy, going along minding my own business and not looking for trouble, and it takes a lot to get me sore, but I'm sore about this case, and what I mean is, I'm good and sore. Maybe I'm just a dumb cop. All right, so I'm a dumb cop. But by God, I'm gonna find out who shot that guy and took him up to Lincoln Park."

"I sure wish you luck," Malone said heartily and hoped that heaven would forgive him.

"I'm gonna fine-toothcomb that guy's life and find out why he came to Chicago. Somebody knows why, and I'm gonna find out. I'm gonna plaster his picture all over the papers. Somebody's gonna remember seeing him. I'm gonna find out where he went when he left the Drake if it's the last damn thing I ever get done." He set his jaw hard. "I don't care how long it takes, either. And don't think I can't do it, because I can. I'm sore about this, that's all. It ain't right for people to do things like this to me, and I'm God damned if I'm gonna stand for it."

Malone remembered past instances of Von Flanagan's dogged persistence when his ire was roused, and decided that the next few days were going to be busy ones. Still, he tried one hopeful shot.

"You might," he said thoughtfully, "be able to put over that accidental death theory and get the newspapers off your tail."

Von Flanagan shook his head. "Sure I could. But I ain't going to. Not this case." He set his glass down with a thump. "Now, you see what I mean, Malone? It's things like this that make it hard for a fella. Next year I quit, so help me. All you have to do is buy a nice little farm somewhere and get two mink, and then just wait. That's all. We'd better have some more beer."

CHAPTER 19

With good luck," Malone said, "I can get him off with twenty years. I hope you'll wait for him, Helene, he's a nice fella."

He had finished his description of the conference with Von Flanagan. Even Jake looked a little concerned.

The lawyer sighed. "Well, you've heard what Von Flanagan is going to do. Maybe we'd better get in ahead of him. I mean we'd better find out who murdered the late Mr. Givvus of Philadelphia. Yes, I think maybe we better had."

There was a little silence.

"Mr. Givvus," Malone said thoughtfully, seems so perfectly the average successful citizen that it's hard to believe he existed. I looked at his picture. An ordinary little guy. I looked up his life, courtesy of Von Flanagan's department. He was a pretty good soapmaker. Member of a good second-rate club. Expensive house in a Philly suburb, probably a very architectural-looking house somewhat on the ornate side. Wife and two kids. Wife president of a garden club. Kids out of college, living on the old man. Girl friend who used to be a private secretary—not his private secretary, someone else's. Shows the man had taste. Not much to live for though. Still, not much reason for anybody to shoot him."

He paused, paced up and down the floor leaving little piles of cigar ash on the rug.

"Funny. Not much reason for anybody to shoot him. But somebody did."

Another silence, a few more trips back and forth on the floor. In his strolling the little lawyer suddenly noticed the odd-shaped contraption of wood, leather, and rubber lying on the table. He picked it up, idly fiddled with it, half-unconsciously.

Suddenly the quiet was shattered by the sound of a gunshot. Jake jumped. Helene screamed. Malone dropped the contraption as though it had turned and bitten him.

"What the hell," he said dazedly, and again, "what the hell!"

"You shot off the sound effect," Jake gasped as soon as words came back to him.

Malone picked it up, looked at it, experimented with it, and shot it off again, this time with less disastrous results, and looked questioningly and dubiously at Helene.

"It's Krause's sound effect," Jake explained. "Helene stole it to conduct an experiment. She's going to send it back." He described the experiment and its results.

"So," Helene added, "It must have been a gun with a silencer, and that means—"

"Wait a minute," the lawyer said excitedly, "wait a minute." He stared at them a moment, walked to the window and looked out, picked up the sound effect and laid it down again, took out a cigar and lighted it, made two more turns up and down the room.

"Malone," Helene said, near-desperation in her voice, "what goes on?"

"I heard Nelle's program last week," Malone said, "and I heard about five minutes of the program that followed it. Jake, what was that program?"

"True Gang Stories, or some such title," Jake said promptly.

"And didn't you tell me the radio was going full blast in Paul March's apartment when you walked in and found the body?"

"It was!" Jake said, a sudden light flickering in his eyes. "Hell's bells yes, you might be right. Last week's Gang Stories script was full of shooting. No one would have noticed one more shot. Anyone who heard it would have assumed it was one of Krause's sound effects coming over the air."

Helene said, "Wonderful! What of it?"

Jake ignored her. "If that's right," he said, "it fixes the time of the shooting very nicely. Somewhere in the half-hour right after the Nelle Brown Revue."

They stared at each other.

"But during the audition," Helene began, "I mean, when Mr. Givvus was killed—how about the sound of the shot then?"

This time it was Jake who paced the floor. Halfway in the eighth lap he paused suddenly, began looking around the room.

"Newspapers," he said, "I want newspapers. Yesterday's newspapers."

Helene unearthed one in the wastebasket. He spread it out on the floor, found the radio page, ran a forefinger down the afternoon's listings.

"Just before the audition," he said slowly, "just a very few minutes before we got the audition underway, The Rider of the Rockies came on the air. The reception-room speaker was probably turned on for it. It—The Rider of the Rockies—has a standard opening."

He paused for thought.

"It opens," he said slowly, "with an Indian war whoop, a burst of galloping hoofbeats"—he produced a highly realistic sound of hoofbeats by patting his thighs with his cupped hands—"and a regular fusillade of gunshots. Boom-boom-tiddy-boom-boom-boom!" He grabbed the sound effect, shot it off a half-dozen times in rapid succession.

Before anyone had a chance to speak, there were running footsteps in the hall. Jake opened the door, stuck his head out, said, "It's all right, Molly, it's just me shooting at my girl," and shut the door again. The footsteps went away.

"All of which means," Malone said, "it didn't need to be a gun with a silencer. The sound of the shot was covered in both cases."

"Lovely," Jake commented, "now all we need to know is who fired the shots."

Malone sighed. "Here are some more trains of thought. First, that the same person committed both murders. That thought has two subdivisions: (*a*) that someone committed both murders thinking that Mr. Givvus was St. John, and (*b*) that someone committed both murders thinking that Mr. Givvus was Mr. Givvus. Then there is the thought that these are two different and totally unrelated crimes, with the same two subdivisions relating to the second murder: (*a*) that the murderer thought he was shooting St. John, and (*b*) that he thought he was shooting Mr. Givvus."

"And subdivision (*c*)," Helene said, "that it was Krause thinking Mr. Givvus had stolen his sound effect."

No one paid any attention to her.

"What I want to know now is," Malone said, looking hopelessly around for his hat, "could this guy have been mistaken for St. John? I've seen his picture. I want to see St. John." He finally located the hat under a crumpled newspaper beside the table. "Get on your horses. We're going to call on St. John."

They were down the stairs, in the car, and halfway down Michigan Avenue before Helene caught enough breath to ask, "But why are we going to see St. John?"

"I want to get a good look at him," Malone told her.

"I'm better-looking than he is," Jake said coyly.

"You are not," Helene said. "St. John is a good-looking guy. Dignified. Impressive. English tweeds and a curved-stem pipe, and a hunting dog curled at his feet before the fireplace."

"He has bunions," Jake said. "Don't forget St. John believes you're my confidential secretary."

"A confidential secretary," Malone said scornfully, "in a simple little gray linen dress that's a Paris import."

"How do you know a Paris import when you see it?" Helene asked, turning into Wacker Drive.

Malone said irritably, "Ask my secretary. She pays my private bills for me out of my personal account." He sniffed. "Well, if St. John wonders about the clothes Jake's secretary is wearing, you can think of the answer."

"I'll tell him my lawyer buys her clothes for her," Jake said.

The usual collection of hopeful actresses, actors, and script writers were waiting to see the great John St. John, but the red-haired girl at the switchboard beamed at Jake and sent the three in without waiting. St. John seemed pale and very tired.

"Sleep well?" Jake inquired pleasantly, sinking into a comfortable red-leather chair. He admired the purplish swelling on St. John's slender and aristocratic nose.

"Excellently," St. John said. He didn't look it.

Malone looked at him closely, walked around the desk and looked at his profile, walked back and stared at him fullface, then took a folded newspaper from his pocket and stared at a picture of the late Mr. Givvus.

"No, Jake," he said, "I think you're wrong. No one could have mistaken Mr. Givvus for this guy."

"Even in a dim light?" Jake asked.

"Even in the dark," Malone said. "Look at this guy's forehead, and then look at Mr. Givvus. St. John here has a wave of hair that comes down this way, and Givvus was half bald. St. John has a long, thin, horsy face, and Givvus was almost round-faced."

"Maybe you're right," Jake said, "but it was an idea anyway."

"They don't look anything alike," Helene said. "But there still doesn't seem to be any motive for anybody shooting Mr. Givvus."

St. John cleared his throat delicately. "I don't mind your using my office for a conference room," he said pleasantly. "But I was under the impression you came up here to see me."

"We did," Malone said, "it just slipped my mind for the moment. How many people knew that your client, Mr. Givvus, was having a secret audition yesterday?"

St. John raised his right eyebrow half an inch. "Wouldn't it be safer to let the murder of Mr. Givvus rest in peace? After all, I'm the only person who seems to have lost anything by it, and God knows, I'm willing to let the whole thing drop."

"I don't want to just let it drop," Malone said. "I want to see it buried. That's why I asked the question."

"Well," St. John said thoughtfully, "well, there was Nelle—and these two people, of course." He nodded toward Jake and Helene. "In addition—Oscar, Schultz, and Ross from the broadcasting company's sales department. Yesterday I told Ross that my client didn't show up for the audition at the last minute. He sympathized with me and, as far as I know, he believed me."

"How about Lou Silver?" Jake asked. "And the band boys and the cast?"

"None of them knew who the audition was for."

"Marvelous," Jake said. "A scene beautifully set for murder. Just as if it had been planned."

"Are you insinuating anything?" St. John asked in a perfectly expressionless voice, raising the other eyebrow.

"No," Jake said nastily, "should I be?"

"Never mind," Malone said. "Look here, St. John. You're positive no one else knew he was going to be there? It's damned important."

"Positive," St. John said wearily, slipping off one shoe under the desk. "I met him at the elevator myself and showed him into the client's room. Outside of the elevator man, no one saw him, and those elevators are carrying up hundreds of people all day long."

"Well then," Malone said, "it's fairly certain that no one will find out Givvus was shot in the client's room, and his body moved to Lincoln Park. That's all I was worrying about."

"Of course," St. John said icily, "murder is murder, and moving a body may be a serious offense."

"So is withholding evidence," Malone said, picking up his hat. "You aren't in the clear either. But I don't give a hoot who murdered the guy. I'm not on the police force. My business is keeping or getting people out of trouble. I'm good at it, too. Any time you are involved in a murder, St. John, here's my card."

He nodded to Jake and Helene, and they left together. St. John's secretary passed them in the doorway, carrying a pile of scripts and a handful of telegrams, and as the door closed, they could hear St. John's tired and harassed voice saying, "Oh God, why do I have to look after *everything—*"

"Poor guy," Helene murmured.

"We didn't find out much," Malone said, "but we and St. John seem to have each other nicely blockaded. He can't tell the world about the letters Nelle wrote Paul March, because if he did, we could tell the world about Givvus being murdered in the client's room, and get him in a heluva jam. That item also works the other way. So right now nobody can make the first move."

"Never a dull moment with the Nelle Brown Revue," Jake commented. "But it would simplify everything if somebody would shoot St. John. Maybe if we wait long enough, Essie St. John will. Now let's me and Helene go to Crown Point and get married. This looks like a nice day for it."

CHAPTER 20

I'm going home and change my dress first," Helene complained. "If I'm really going to get married, I've got to dress up for it."

Malone said, "I can get you married at Crown Point any time up to midnight. Helene can change her dress, we'll have dinner, and I'll go along and get you married. I'll be the best man and bridesmaid all at once. I'll even buy the gin."

"All right," Jake said with a long sigh, "but I'm beginning to have a feeling the wedding will be held in the old people's home."

They drove back to Erie Street. In Helene's apartment they found Nelle and Baby sitting side by side on the davenport.

"The door was open," Nelle explained, "so we came right in. Helene, this is Baby. Baby, this is Helene. We just dropped in to find out if you were really going to get married today."

"That's the intention," Jake said. He saw a speculative gleam in the little lawyer's eye and had an uncomfortable premonition that the plans were due for at least one more postponement.

"I'm glad you dropped in," Malone said happily. "There's just time for us all to have a drink together before taking off for Crown Point." He and Helene vanished into the kitchenette and began concocting a long, cool drink composed largely of gin.

Jake settled down in an easy chair and looked at Baby. Thank God, he thought, he wasn't one of the pretty boys. Good-looking enough, as far as that went. But not handsome. He didn't seem to care whether he was good-looking or not. Probably didn't even know. Rather boyish-looking, Jake decided, and wondered if Nelle was the first important romance in the young man's life.

"No," Baby was saying to Helene, "radio doesn't seem glamorous to me. It's a lot of hard work. But I like it."

Baby would like hard work, Jake thought, and he'd do it, too. He wasn't another Paul March, with ability, but getting by on the strength of his personal charm. By some miracle, Nelle had picked wisely this time.

"Did you ever know a man in radio named Paul March?" Helene asked very innocently. "This used to be his apartment."

Baby wrinkled his brow a little. Jake was glad he was looking away from Nelle's too-expressionless face. "Paul March. Yes, I did. I did some work for him on a daytime serial a few months ago. He does nice work. I never knew him very well."

It sounded genuine enough.

Malone led the conversation away from Paul March, and Jake went on thinking about Nelle Brown and Baby. He was trying to foresee how it would end. Baby was taking it hard, that was obvious. A lot of gin would flow under the bridgework, but it would be a long long time before Baby would forget Nelle Brown. Too bad. But what about Nelle? Jake sighed. Somehow he had the feeling that the ending would be very, very sad.

Malone was talking about the mysterious murder of a Mr. Givvus on a Lincoln Park bench.

Baby's eyes brightened. "Say, I used to work for him. Never thought of it before, but he's the same guy."

"Honestly?" Helene said, wide-eyed.

"Sure thing," Baby told her. "He had a local program on the air in Philly, and I drew the assignment. But he thought I was lousy, and I got the gate. That's what sent me here to Chicago."

"Well, well," Jake said, "and it must have been a difficult trick, sneaking up on that park bench to shoot him."

Baby grinned. "Oh, I didn't have any trouble. I snuck up on him, silentlike. You see, I'm really a full-blooded Cherokee Indian, with my hair bleached."

"Speaking of hair bleach," Helene said, "let's have another drink."

If Baby had actually murdered Givvus, Jake wondered, would he be smart enough to know that was exactly the right thing to say? But why the hell would Baby—

They talked of murder, Mr. Givvus, Philadelphia, radio, and cocktail recipes for the time it took to consume two more of the long, cool drinks. Then Jake had a flash of inspiration.

"Say, where were you all yesterday afternoon?" he asked Baby. "Oscar was giving a special audition and thought he might have to use you if someone fell out of the cast."

"Yesterday?" Baby thought for a minute. "I did a commercial at one-fifteen and I was on a show later in the afternoon."

"Was it The Rider of the Rockies?" Jake asked very casually.

Baby shook his head. "No. I'm in today's script though." He looked at his watch. "Got to leave pretty quick, too. Funny my landlady didn't tell you where to reach me yesterday. I had a couple of hours between broadcasts."

"She probably forgot," Jake said. "But I should have run into you around the studios. I was there all afternoon."

"I went back in the announcer's room and took a nap," Baby said.

He declined another drink, explaining that he had a show to do; the rest decided there was time for one more, and while it was being made, Nelle and Helene disappeared into the bathroom. As soon as they were out of earshot, Baby turned to Jake, his young face suddenly grave.

"Say, is something worrying Nelle?"

Jake shook his head. "Not that I know. Why?"

"I don't know. I thought she looked tired and a little pale. I guess things are never very easy for her." He scowled. "I know I'm not very important to her, but I mean to stick around as long as she needs me."

"Why?" Jake asked, "if you're not important to her?"

"This sounds funny," Baby said, "but look. Nelle's going to need me very much someday. It's like this. I know just how much Tootz means to her. He means a hell of a lot. He's foundation, if you know what I mean."

Jake nodded, and said, "Sure."

"Tootz isn't going to live forever. He's getting on. When it happens it's going to be a terrible blow to Nelle. I want to be there to catch her when it comes. Oh, I don't mean marry her. I'm just another guy to Nelle. But when something like that happens, if somebody like me just happens to be there, if you know what I mean."

"Sure," Jake said again, wishing he had taken either one more drink or one less.

"Another thing," Baby said, "this March guy. I didn't want to say so in front of Nelle, but I knew all about—you-know-what-I-mean—"

Jake nodded and reflected that radio announcers should always have their personal conversations as well as their script written for them.

"March told me," Baby went on. "I got to know him better than I told Nelle. One night he got drunk, got to bragging about her, and I popped him one, the sonofabitch. If he ever shoots off about her again, I'll break his neck. Only I didn't want Nelle to know that I knew that. Because it would make her feel bad." He drew a long breath. "It's like this. I don't care about anything she's done in the past, or what she's still going to do in the future. For this little space in between, she's my life That sounds like something from a lousy script, but I mean it just that way. She's my life."

That was when Nelle and Helene returned.

Baby discovered it was time to leave for rehearsal, said good-by all around, made arrangements to meet Nelle later, and went away.

"There," said Malone, who had overheard the conversation from the kitchenette, "is a young man who would not only give you the shirt off his back, Nelle, but throw in his necktie and vest as well."

Jake remembered something he had wanted to ask Nelle for a long time. It was wonderful how gin made him remember things.

He looked at her very seriously. "Nelle. Why? I mean, what do you see in Baby? What did you see in Paul March?"

Her eyes suddenly seemed to become very large, and to see something that the rest of them could not see. "Love. Don't laugh at me. I keep looking for it and thinking it's going to happen, and then it doesn't. People—like Paul—they happen, and I think, this time this is it, this time this is love, and then I find out it isn't. I know it can happen, because it happens to other people, but never to me. I want someone to be my whole life so that nothing else is important to me, and no one ever is. Other people fall in love and it goes on forever and ever, but me, I know it's just pretending. Or perhaps it's me who knows what's real and the other people are just pretending. I don't know. Perhaps you can't understand, but it's like a kind of ideal that I keep on looking for, even when I know it doesn't exist and I'll never find it. And when I sing a love song, I'm not singing it to someone real, someone I love today or this week or this year, but to the ideal even when I know he isn't anywhere."

"Oh boy," Jake said, "oh boy, how that could have been worked into a script!"

The dreamy look was gone in a flash. "Oh Jake," she wailed. "I wish you'd written it down while I was saying it!"

He leaned back in his chair and stared at her admiringly. "There's the reason it never happens to you. To other people, ordinary people, your singing and your acting is make-believe and the rest of life is real. But to you, the world is make-believe." He sighed. "Months now I've tried to understand you and now I do. It's because you're an artist. It took Malone's gin to make me see it, but now I do."

Malone said very severely. "Let's all us artists have one more drink."

Nelle refused, explaining that she had to go, since Tootz expected her home. She kissed them all good-by and left, after wishing Jake and Helene a happy marriage for the third time in two days.

"That reminds me," Helene said severely. "You two seem to have forgotten it, but—"

Jake rose to his feet. "I have not forgotten it. This time we go to Crown Point. Nothing stands in the way."

It was then that the telephone call came from Essie St. John.

CHAPTER 21

"Oh, thank God, Jake," Essie St. John said over the wire. "I've been trying everywhere to reach you, and finally I thought of calling Nelle's, and the butler suggested that I call this number, and here you are. I'm so glad I found you."

"I'm glad you're glad," Jake said. "Is that what you wanted to know?"

"I can't tell you over the phone, Jake, I've got to see you."

He groaned. "Listen, Essie. For two days now I've been trying to—"

"Jake, this is terribly important. I've simply got to see you. It's something that I've found out and you've got to know about it. It's important, I tell you. Oh Jake, it won't take five minutes."

"Well, where can I meet you?"

"Somewhere. I'm in the lobby of your hotel but I don't want to wait here for you. I'm so afraid someone will see me."

"My God," he said, "what *is* up?"

"Jake, I can't talk here."

"Well—" he thought for a moment. "Essie, my room number is 1217. Romp up there and wait in the hall. I'll be along in a couple of minutes and we can talk up in my room. No matter what the trouble is, pull yourself together."

He hung up, swearing softly. Lord only knew what was the matter with Essie St. John. Whatever it was, he probably wasn't going to like it. He climbed the stairs to Helene's apartment and explained what had happened.

"Something terribly important," Malone repeated. "Probably she wants to tell you that she murdered Paul March and stored his body in a trunk and then murdered Mr. Givvus just to keep her hand in."

"Probably she wants to tell me she can't go on living with St. John any longer," Jake said gloomily. "Well, I'll find out."

"A fine thing," Helene said indignantly. "You put off marrying me to go meet another dame. What are you going to do, Malone?"

The little lawyer sighed and stretched. "Go see Von Flanagan once more just to keep us on the safe side of things. Maybe I'll have dinner with him, and meet you later."

"He must think he's getting popular all of a sudden," Jake said. "I hope he doesn't begin to wonder about it."

Malone said, "I hope he doesn't sell me a mink ranch." He picked up his hat. "Helene, give us a ride."

She drove Jake to his hotel, made arrangements to meet him later, and left to drive Malone to Von Flanagan's office. Jake looked at his watch, resolved that it was going to take a very short time to dispose of Essie St. John's troubles, whatever they were. As he passed through the lobby, he remembered the tremor of her voice over the telephone and paused in the drugstore for a couple of pints of rye; one, he reflected, for Essie, and one for emergencies.

He found her pacing the corridor in front of his room, her friendly, plain face pale and strained. Without a word he opened his door, shoved her inside and into a chair, uncapped one of the bottles, poured a drink, and put it into her hand.

"Thanks, Jake." She loosened her fur and let it fall to the floor, kicked off one shoe. "Oh Jake, he's terrible."

"Take the drink first."

She gulped it down, reached for the cigarette he handed her.

"Jake, I found out all about it. About his having those letters. Do you know what I'm talking about?"

"I might if you keep on talking."

He wondered if she knew Paul March was dead.

"Somehow he got Paul to give them to him. I don't know how, but anyway he's got them. Jake, he's—"

"He's terrible," Jake said, filling her glass again. "How did you find out about the letters?"

"He was taking a bath," Essie said. "I mean, I knew he was up to something, and when he was taking a bath I looked through the pockets of all his clothes. And I found the letters. They're in his inside coat pocket. I just looked at them and I knew right away what he was doing with them."

"Oh God," Jake moaned, "if only you'd had the inspiration to steal them and burn them up!"

"I didn't dare, Jake. You don't know what he might have done when he found out about it. I didn't dare. But I'm going to get them. I haven't finished telling you about it yet." She finished the drink and set the glass down on the floor. "Yes, I'm going to get those letters for you, Jake. I won't let him get away with this. It isn't fair, that's what. It isn't fair."

"Very nice, even noble," Jake said, "but how are you going to do it?"

"He thinks I'm going to be away tonight, Jake. He thinks I'm staying out in Kenilworth with Jane—you know, my sister. Jane is swell about things, you know. If I'm supposed to be staying there and he should phone, the maid says that Jane and I have gone to the movies, and she'll tell me when I get back. Then Jane calls me up where I am, and I call up John. It's really somebody special, too, Jake. I mean it isn't just one of those things. This is love, Jake."

"Look here," he said, looking at his watch, this is very interesting but I haven't time to listen to all your personal life."

"Of course, but Jake, you don't think I'm perfectly awful to do something like this, when John is—well, like he is? It sort of makes me happier, if you know what I mean. And it isn't the same as if he—John—

was—I mean, if he was interested in me that way."

"I can't imagine anybody not being interested in you that way," Jake said gallantly.

She blushed unbecomingly. "It isn't me, it's just women." She said, "I mean he hasn't just lost interest in me, it's that—well, not anybody," she finished lamely.

"Proving that bunions are not an aphrodisiac," Jake said. He picked up her glass and set it on the dresser. "But what about the letters?"

"I was just getting to that," she said. "He thinks I'm staying with Jane tonight."

"And you aren't," he said.

She blushed again. Jake noticed that her nose was a little shiny.

"Well, never mind," Jake said, "go on."

"I thought of how I could get the letters for you. The maid is out tonight, and he'll be all alone in the house. Before I left, we had a drink together, and I doped him."

"My God, Essie!"

"It's some stuff I got once from a friend of mine, a druggist. It won't hurt him, but it'll knock him out cold. When I'm sure it's had time to put him to sleep, I'll go back to the house and get the letters out of his pocket. He won't know who did it, and he'll think I was at Jane's all the time. She'll swear I was."

"Essie, you're a superwoman. How did you ever think of it?"

"I've developed a pretty good head for thinking of things," she said unhappily.

"I know." He dropped a hand on her shoulder.

"Jake, after I get the letters, what shall I do with them? I don't dare carry them around with me."

"Wrap them up and leave them at the desk downstairs. I'd meet you, but I've—got a date. Essie, are you sure this won't get you into trouble?"

"I'm sure of it, Jake. I'd take a chance even if it would. But—" she looked at her watch. "In a few hours he'll be dead to the world. I'll go out there and get it all fixed up, and then I'll leave the letters here for you."

"Essie," he told her, "this means so damned much to Nelle. You just don't know how much. You're a swell guy."

"I like Nelle," she said simply, "I like Nelle, and I like you, and don't thank me, Jake. I owe you something for popping John one on the beak."

Jake grinned. "Nobody needs to thank me for that."

It would be a dirty trick under the circumstances, but he wondered if he could learn anything from Essie. He poured another drink for her, pouring one for himself at the same time, sat down beside her cozily.

"Essie dear, how was it about Paul March?"

She blinked a little. "What do you mean? You mean—Paul and me?"

"Well—yes. Paul and you. H'm?"

"I—don't know. I knew that Nelle—but you knew that too, didn't you? I thought he was a louse to treat Nelle the way he did, but he was pretty much on the make with Paul March's interests at heart. I did have a few dates with him. He had a certain appeal." She chose her words meticulously, her eyes on the carpet.

"He must have had," Jake said, and very casually, "seen him lately?"

She shook her head. "Not for weeks. He went to lunch with me quite a long time ago and borrowed some money from me. I guess he was pretty hard up. And I haven't seen him since."

Jake nodded slowly and thoughtfully. "It's just as well. I can't give Paul very much. He's almost in the class with your old man."

"I wouldn't quite say that, Jake. No. No, not at all. Paul knew he could always make friends, he always felt things were going to be easy for him. He was just plain spoiled, that's all. He'd be on the make for some radio job and get it and do swell stuff for a while, and then he'd think, 'What the hell, what's the use,' and then, boom. Not John. No, he knows people don't like him and it hurts worse than his bunions do."

"I never would have guessed that," Jake said. "I thought he didn't give a damn about anybody."

She frowned. "He's unhappy, Jake. A lot of little stuff. Like his feet. And then he has trouble with his stomach. Not anything serious, just a nuisance. And he gets heat rash. And he knows people don't like him, and just thinks and thinks about it, and then he gets mean."

"I see," Jake said inadequately. He was pretty sure now that Essie St. John didn't know Paul March was dead.

"I think he wants to be a great success so that all the people who don't like him will wish they did," Essie said.

He slipped an arm around her shoulders. "Essie, why did you marry him?"

"I don't know. I guess because nobody else had ever asked me as if he meant it. I'm not very good-looking, you know. But I do have money. That's why he wanted to marry me, but he was smart enough not to let me know until it was too late." She stood up wearily and a trifle unsteadily, adjusting her fur. "Well, I'm off. Wish me luck."

"You're a brave babe. I'll be looking for Nelle's love notes in the morning."

She tried to smile. He kissed her good-by very tenderly at the door, not especially wanting to, but feeling that she might like it. Then he watched her marching down the hall, thinking how superb her figure looked from the back, and what a shame it was that St. John didn't appreciate it.

There was time for a quick shower before he went to meet Helene. He bathed hurriedly, put on a fresh suit, and brushed his hair, whistling happily. He stowed the unopened bottle of rye in his pocket, observed that an inch was left in the other one, and poured it down his throat.

Essie was going to get those letters back, good old Essie. Malone was nuts. Nobody gave a hoot who murdered Paul March or Mr. Givvus. Goldman would re-sign the contract with a flourish the night of the broadcast. Everything was smooth, serene, and settled. Everything was perfect. And he and Helene were going to be married in a few hours.

It was just a great big beautiful world.

CHAPTER 22

Jake found Helene listening to a new installment of Molly Coppins' life story. The evening was very warm, and she had changed into a dress that reminded him a little of a cloud, very faintly gray, almost misty. She greeted him enthusiastically.

"Five more minutes and I'd have married Malone. What have you been drinking?"

"Rye."

"I've been drinking gin. We'd better think of a compromise. While we're waiting for Malone, let's go to Isbell's for dinner."

On the way, he told her what Essie had done and was going to do.

"Marvelous," she said. "Now as long as nobody finds out how Mr. Givvus got moved to Lincoln Park, and Paul March's body doesn't turn up, everything is rosy."

"Somehow I don't anticipate Paul March's body turning up," he told her. "I've an idea St. John has hidden it pretty carefully."

"St. John?"

"Who else? I don't think St. John is a guy who would buy incriminating letters from some bird, and then take a chance on the bird coming back on him for more dough sometime."

She sighed. "Wouldn't it be nice if we could just pin it on him?"

"Wouldn't it be nice if we could just forget the whole thing," Jake said.

He grinned wryly. "Funny thing. Nobody likes St. John except possibly St. John. Nothing would suit us better than to pin Paul March's murder on him. We feel sure he's guilty of it. And damn it, we can't do a thing."

"We can get married," she said, "though that begins to seem just about as impossible. Jake, if St. John murdered Paul March, who murdered Mr. Givvus? Surely not St. John."

"They're different parts of two entirely different things."

"You're drunk. Jake, who murdered Mr. Givvus?"

"I'm not sure, but I think it's part of a gang war."

"You're insane. Who murdered Mr. Givvus?"

"If you must know," he said, "I did. And now shut up about it until after dinner."

During dinner they argued the comparative merits of Erie Street and Jake's hotel as a place to live. At last they left the restaurant and drove slowly toward the lake. A gentle quiet had settled with the darkness over Chicago's near-North Side. A few strollers went up and down Michigan Avenue; on Superior Street people sat on their door steps, smoking and idly chatting. Half a dozen children who should have been in bed hours before played hopscotch under the street lamps. Out on the still lake, the lights of a few boats bobbed up and down. The world was very peaceful and very content.

Jake sighed happily and slid a little closer to Helene. "Is it the world that's terrific or just the rye I've been drinking?"

She said softly, "I've never known which was the real and which was the dream. Jake, are things real when you're drunk or when you're sober? Are they real when you're asleep or when you're awake?"

"Quietness is real," he told her. "Only that. The world was never as quiet as it is tonight."

They drove in silence to Oak Street beach, went around the block, and started back along the Drive.

"In another hour it'll be time to meet Malone," Jake said. "He said he could get us married in Crown Point any time up to midnight."

"I'll believe it when we get there," she said direly.

"Helene, are you sure you want to do it? It must take a lot of nerve to marry me."

"It doesn't take nerve," she said, "but it does seem to take time. I wonder how Malone is making out."

"He's probably finding out things that Von Flanagan doesn't even realize he knows."

They watched the lights on Navy Pier weaving a gold-laced veil over the water, finally turned off the drive onto a dark street lined with smallish factory buildings and warehouses.

"There's Tootz' warehouse," Jake said, pointing to a dark, three-story building.

"Where he keeps the hay for his horses?" she asked, peering at it curiously.

"No, it really is his warehouse. All that was left from the crash. Somehow he hung onto it."

She drove on to the end of the street, turned around, and came slowly back.

"Why isn't it used for something?"

"I don't know. Some guy was making experiments there with a new kind of refrigeration for fruits. Built a swell freezing chamber, and then went broke and quit. We gave a party there once."

"The kind of party that calls for refrigeration?" she asked.

"All of that." He added a few details.

She slowed down suddenly, as suddenly stopped.

"Jake, if I'm not mistaken, there's something going on there now that calls for refrigeration."

"What are you talking about?"

"Look."

He looked in the direction of the warehouse, jumped out of the car, ran across the walk, and peered in through the window. She followed him.

"What is it, Jake?"

"Looks like a fire. Not much of one, but a fire. We'd better go in and investigate."

"We'd better send an alarm."

"I want to take a look first."

He rattled the door, finally picked up a stone from the gutter, broke the window glass, reached his arm inside, and turned the latch. The door swung open. Through the darkness they could see a faint reddish flickering far in the back of the building.

"Helene, please wait here."

"No. I'm coming with you."

There was no time to stop and argue about it. He plunged into the darkness of the deserted building, Helene close behind him. Suddenly a rat scuttled across their path, and she screamed.

"Afraid of mice!" he flung back at her.

"That was no mouse," she gasped. "It was a monster. Three feet long and eyes like balls of fire—*Jake!*"

"I see it," he said. Ahead of them the reddish flickering grew higher, brighter.

"No. On the floor!"

In the faint light they could see that the dust on the floor had been disturbed. The trail led through the cobwebs to a great white door. Jake raced to the door, tugged at it frantically, it opened a tiny way and fell shut again. He made one more gasping, desperate effort and it suddenly opened wide, fell back against the wall, and stayed there.

The faint reddish light, mingling with a bluish glare through the dusty windows, poured into a little white room, eerie and strange with its arrangements of odd-shaped pipes and tubes. Against its glaring whiteness, the thing on the floor seemed terribly dark.

In one swift movement Jake bent forward, turned it over. He stared at it, forgetting the fire that was crackling closer now.

"We've found Paul March!"

CHAPTER 23

There was the body of Paul March on the floor, and there was the fire crackling and spreading. The thing to do, Jake agreed later, was to go away, drive away as fast as Helene's car would go, let the fire destroy the evidence of some unknown person's crime.

That was what he thought later. But at the moment, the thing on the warehouse floor was the body of a man, and the fire was coming closer. Hardly conscious of what he was doing, he lifted it from the floor. It was cold, and terribly hard, like ice. For the first time, he was aware of the almost obscene coldness of the refrigerating chamber.

"Jake, what are you going to do?"

"Get this out of here. Race out to the car, drive it into the alley—quick, Helene."

She disappeared into the cavernous darkness like a frightened hare. He lifted the body over his shoulder, staggering under its weight. The smoke filled the warehouse now; choking and gasping, he made his way to a window on the alley side. As he reached it, he saw Helene's long, sleek car turn into the alley, drive up, and stop.

He leaned the body against the wall while he struggled with the window and finally flung it open. One cautious look into the darkness of the alley, then he lifted the body through the opening, and climbed after it.

It was then that he began to wonder what he was doing.

In the distance he could hear the sound of a siren. Someone else had seen the warehouse fire.

There was no time to spend considering alternatives. Helene opened the door to the back of the car; Jake stowed the body of Paul March on the floor and carefully covered it with the rug. Then he climbed in beside Helene, slammed the door, and the big car backed down the alley. The wailing sirens were very close now.

"We should have gone straight ahead and turned down the other street," Helene said grimly. "But it's too late."

They reached the corner in time to find it blocked by fire apparatus. A fireman swore at them irritably for being in the way. Finally, with no little maneuvering, they were free again. Beyond the corner, Helene stopped, close to the curb.

"Helene, for the love of heaven, get out of here."

She switched off the engine. "No. That fireman noticed the car. If we drive away, he may get suspicious. If we park here and pretend we're watching the fire, he'll forget about it."

In a more sober moment he might have found a few flaws in her reasoning, but he could think of none at the time. He followed her down the street to where a little crowd had already gathered. The old building was blazing merrily now; great tongues of flame shot up into the night sky; dense clouds of smoke veiled the buildings near by. Now and then firemen appeared briefly on the roof and vanished again.

"Oh boy!" said a young man next to Jake. "She's a dandy!"

To the indescribable delight of the crowd, the water tower came into position and shot foaming ribbons into the upper windows. There was a moment of almost unbearable excitement when a fireman, overcome by smoke, was carried down a ladder from the roof. A woman in the crowd began screaming and was led away. Picture trucks arrived from the newspapers and bursts of white light from the photographers' flashlights illumined the burning building. A police squad car whined dismally around the corners.

Suddenly the roof and part of a wall caved in with a resounding crash, sending clouds of dust and small debris to mingle with the smoke. Flames began to appear at every window, and policemen started moving the crowd farther away from the scene.

Without warning, there was a deafening roar, a flood of blinding light, a few moments of frantic activity. A moment later a sheet of flame turned the street as bright as day. In that instant a woman in the crowd screamed suddenly and clutched at a policeman.

"There she is!" she shrieked, pointing at Helene. "I saw her here when it started. She's a pyromaniac. I heard a man with her say—"

It was the black-haired waitress from Rickett's.

Helene turned and ran like a deer toward the car. Jake ran after her with a wild thought of stopping her and making explanations. But before he could catch up with her, she had leaped into the front seat and started the motor. He jumped in beside her and slammed the door shut just as the big car bounded forward. Looking back, he could see the policeman running hopelessly after them.

"Helene," he cried, "Helene, you can't do this—"

She paid no attention. The car raced down the dark street, swung north for a block, took a corner on two wheels, another block, and turned onto Michigan Avenue. In the distance Jake could hear the siren of the squad car.

"Helene, stop—we can explain—"

She said grimly, "You forget we have a passenger."

It was very late and Michigan Avenue was almost deserted. They sped through a stop light, reached the approach to the bridge. Suddenly ahead of them they heard bells clanging.

"You can't make it, the bridge is going up."

It was only the first warning bell, the barrier at the bridge was just beginning to move. She put on added speed, heading straight at the bridge. Someone near it ran into the street, waving at her frantically. The wailing siren was coming nearer now.

In one last burst of speed she crossed the bridge, missing the last barrier by a hair's breadth. Jake could see it settle into place as she sped on down the avenue.

"Just like the movies," she gasped, "they on one side of the bridge and we on the other."

"Helene, you can't possibly get away—"

"Shut up," she said, "I'm trying to think."

She turned onto a side street, turned again and drove up an alley, made another turn, and entered the labyrinth of underground passages known as the lower level. Skillfully she maneuvered the big car into the cavernous street that was directly below Michigan Avenue, and drove straight to the double-decked bridge. It was still up, and she paused at the barrier.

"When the bridge goes down, they'll be crossing south on the top of it," she said, "and we'll be crossing north on the bottom. Not bad, eh? A neat trick."

"A neat trick," Jake repeated angrily, "and then what? By this time a description of you and of this car is going out over the police radio into every squad car in the city."

"I'd leave the car somewhere," she said thoughtfully, "but they'd find it and find the passenger."

A boat whistled mournfully passing the bridge, and went on down the Chicago River. The bridge began to go down, slowly, importantly, majestically; finally, it settled into place with a little shiver. The bell clanged for another moment while the barrier lifted.

As they drove across, they could hear the police siren wailing above them.

"What are you going to do?"

"Keep driving on streets the squad cars haven't even heard about," she told him.

She turned into a dark, deserted passage just beyond the bridge, drove west a few blocks, turned north again. There was not another car in sight; the street was lined with unlighted factory buildings.

"Jake, I've got to have a drink."

In the semidarkness he could see how pale she was. He remembered the bottle of rye, uncapped it, and held it to her lips.

"Jake, who took him there, and why? And what are we going to do with him?"

"I don't know. He's our story and we're stuck with him."

"Who would have known about the refrigerating room?"

"I knew, and Nelle, of course, and Tootz, and everybody connected with the show. You see, last year, just about this time, we gave a party for the cast. It was hotter than the hinges of hell, and somebody thought of what a bright idea it would be to throw the party in the old abandoned warehouse, with the refrigerating device going. It worked swell."

"But why take *him* there?"

"Can you think, offhand, of a better place?"

She thought for a moment. "Outside of a park bench, no."

Again he held the bottle to her lips.

"He's an ingenious devil," she remarked at last.

"Who?" Jake asked a little stupidly.

"St. John, of course. Who else?"

It was his turn to be silent.

"There can't be any doubt but what St. John shot him," she said after a while. "You said so yourself. And the person who shot him must have been the person who moved the body. The question in my mind is, why did he bother to move it?"

"He didn't want the body to be found," Jake said slowly, "because then his possession of the letters would automatically point to him as March's murderer. He was counting on the fact that everybody would believe March had left Chicago, and nobody would know about the murder."

"Then why not just dispose of the body so that it wouldn't be found?"

"Ever try disposing of a body so it won't be found?" Jake asked. "It isn't as easy as it sounds. Besides, he might have had a reason for wanting the body where he could produce it."

"Why, Jake?"

"So that if anything happened to the letters that were his hold over Nelle, he could use Paul March's murder for the same purpose."

She shivered.

"It was a perfect place to hide the body," Jake said thoughtfully. "And naturally St. John would know about it, having been at the party. It would be easy as pie to break into the building, and not a Chinaman's chance that anybody would blunder in and discover it. We never would have, if the place hadn't caught on fire."

She said very slowly, "By this time Essie has swiped the letters. Essie is away from home, and she told you the maid was away for the night. St. John is still deep in a drugged sleep."

"Helene, just what do you propose doing?"

The big car leaped forward in a sudden burst of speed.

"We're going to take the body up to St. John's house and leave it with him," she said happily. "It'll just be our own little present to him, yours and mine!"

CHAPTER 24

"But you can't do that," Jake said in a dazed voice. "It's wrong. It's—it's arson."

"You've got the wrong crime," she told him. "That's what they're chasing me for."

"Well damn it," he said, "anyway it's illegal."

"So is driving around with a murder victim in the back of the car," Helene observed.

He could find no answer to that one.

"Besides," she said after a pause, "it's dangerous. Driving around, I mean."

"True," Jake agreed. "But suppose St. John didn't murder Paul March," he said after a little serious thought.

"Have you the faintest shadow of a doubt about it?" Helene asked.

"Well," Jake said reflectively, "well, no."

She said, "You'd better take a drink."

"That's the first really good idea you've had," Jake said.

"Where does St. John live?" she asked, a few blocks later.

He told her, adding, "But suppose someone catches us in the act of presenting St. John with a frozen stiff. A stiff, frozen stiff," he muttered after a little pause.

"You didn't think of that when you presented Lincoln Park with the late Mr. Givvus," she said irritably.

That was when Jake gave up the argument.

"I hope this fixes St. John's wagon once and for all," she said virtuously. "It's not that I object to his going around murdering people, but I'm getting tired of driving the victims around."

She drove north through an intricate maze of dark and deserted streets, miraculously escaped becoming hopelessly lost, and finally turned into the street where St. John lived. It was quiet and very peaceful. Half a dozen cars were parked in front of buildings here and there, but there were few lights, little motion.

"There's the house, Helene."

The big car slid noiselessly up the driveway, and stopped beside the back porch. Jake stole softly up the steps and tried the door. It was unlocked.

"Where would be a good place to put it?" Helene whispered.

"Somewhere so that the maid will be the one to find him, in the morning. It would be better if someone else rather than St. John discovered the body."

"In the kitchen, then."

Jake looked up and down the street, saw that no one was in sight. Carefully and very quietly, he carried the body of Paul March up the back steps, across the narrow porch, and into the kitchen. On a sudden inspiration he propped it up beside the kitchen door so that it would fall across the floor the instant the door was opened. Then he closed the door silently, and tiptoed back to the car.

"Drive away as quietly as you can."

She backed the car very slowly and gingerly down the driveway, almost without sound.

"Helene, stop a minute."

She obeyed. He laid one hand on her shoulder and pointed toward a lighted window. Through it they could see John St. John, huddled in an easy chair before his radio. In the still night, they could hear the faint sound of dance music coming from the loudspeaker.

"All right—drive on."

She turned out of the driveway and into the dimly lighted street. Jake laughed a little bitterly.

"What amuses you?"

"I was thinking of St. John, imagining that he has Nelle's letters in his pocket, Paul March's body safely hidden away where it will never be found, and everything all serene. Picture him waking up tomorrow to find that the letters are gone, heaven knows how or where, and the maid coming in saying, 'Scuse me fo' disturbin' you, Mist' St. John, but they's a daid man in the kitchen.' "

"Your blackface accent is terrible," she commented. "Picture Essie St. John finding out that St. John has gone to the jug, and she won't have to live with him any more. Picture Nelle finding out that the letters are out of the way. Jake, do you feel like a boy scout?"

"I feel like a troop of boy scouts."

"I'm beginning to feel like a fugitive," she said meditatively. "What are we going to do about all these policemen looking for me?"

He swore irritably. "I'd forgotten that for the moment." He was silent, thinking fast. "The first thing is to get rid of the car. This fancy gas buggy of yours can be spotted a mile away."

"So if you think I'm going to sink it in the lake, you're crazy."

"Don't interrupt me. I know a garage where it'll be safe. Know the garage man." He gave her the address, near Lincoln Park.

"I hate to do this," she said. "I feel like a lost child without the car."

"You'll get it back in a day or so. Malone can straighten this out for you. As I've said before, what have we got a lawyer for?"

She drove to the address Jake had given her, parked the car in an alley while he went in to make arrangements. A few minutes later he returned, accompanied by a heavy-set man in overalls who nodded to Helene and slid into the driver's seat. She rescued a package of hairpins and the remains of Jake's bottle of rye from the side pocket and watched forlornly while the overalled man drove the car into the darkened garage.

"It'll be safe there," he consoled her. "He'll never let anyone find it as long as the police are out looking for it."

"How did you explain things to him?"

"I told him you'd just assisted in the hijacking of a truck and the cops had gotten a description of the car."

"Thoughtful of you."

"Now we stop at a drugstore and phone Nelle."

They stopped at the first corner. He called Nelle's apartment; no one answered.

"Must be Bigges' night off," he commented. "But I can find Nelle." He thought for a moment, called Baby, found that Nelle was there, and got her on the phone.

"I can't say anything over the phone," he told her, "but I wanted you to know all your troubles are over."

"Jake, are you drunk?" she asked over the wire.

"That's beside the point. Your property, if you know what I mean, has been safely recovered from a gentleman that it didn't belong to."

"Oh, darling!"

"Don't call me darling," he said righteously. "Helene can hear you. Furthermore, another object that was lost has been found, and a crime that was committed will be blamed on the individual who committed it."

"You talk like a swami," she complained.

He caroled happily into the phone, "Way down upon the swami river," and said hastily, "Don't hang up, I just wanted to warn you to be surprised when you read the morning newspapers."

"What are you going to do now?"

"I'm going to get married. Good-by." He hung up, called Malone's hotel, was told that the little lawyer was not in his room nor in the lobby, though a bellhop remembered seeing him sitting in the lobby earlier in the evening.

He looked at his watch. It was nearly three hours past the time when he had promised to meet Malone. He joined Helene at the news counter, found her reading an account of the chase of a blonde woman believed to be a pyromaniac. According to the paper, the woman's car had last been seen on Michigan Avenue, going south, and was believed headed for Hammond, Indiana.

"Nice, fast work," he said admiringly, "both by the papers and by ourselves, though heaven knows why everything gets blamed on Hammond."

"Heaven knows why everything gets blamed on me," she complained.

He looked at her. The pale gray dress was dusty and stained, a cobweb clung to the deep gray wrap. Her hair was pleasantly disheveled; there was a small smudge of dirt across her beautiful nose.

"Your face is dirty and you look like hell, but I still love you. Let's get out of here and into a taxi."

They found a taxi near Lincoln Park, gave the driver the Erie Street address. As they neared the building, a police car passed them, driving slowly. Jake tapped on the glass partition.

"Let us out in the alley. Her husband doesn't know she's out."

The driver nodded sympathetically, turned up the alley, and let them out near the rear of the building.

"Jake, can you get me in safely?"

"I think so. There's any number of ways of getting into this place."

He helped her over a board fence, across a narrow back yard, and through a door that led into the basement. They went a little cautiously past a coalbin and through a furnace room to a narrow flight of wooden stairs.

"Better let me go first to smell out the way. The place might be crawling with cops."

He tiptoed to the top of the stairs. No one was in the halls; the building was quiet and deserted. He motioned to Helene to follow him. There was a light showing faintly above Molly's door, he rapped softly.

"Come in," Molly called.

He led Helene into the room. Molly was sitting by the window, talking with a plump, brunette girl who was dressed lightly and simply in a bright-colored cotton kimono.

"This is Rose," Molly said by way of introduction. "She couldn't sleep and came down to talk to me. My God, what's happened to you? Do you know the police are looking for you?"

"Know it!" Jake said bitterly.

Helene sank into a chair.

Jake told the story of his unfortunate remark in Rickett's, explained that they had innocently gone to watch what looked like a good fire, and gave a few details of the subsequent chase. The plump brunette seemed to find it amusing.

"Thank God it's nothing worse!" Molly said with feeling. "The cops have been all over this place. Someone told them she lived here. They looked at everybody in the building, and made a note of all the apartments where the occupant was out, and said they'd be back later. In fact," she said very calmly, looking out the window "they *are* back."

Helene turned pale. "Oh God. All that chasing around for nothing!"

"Nothing, my eye!" Molly said indignantly. She rose very leisurely, and said, "Rose, you go up in 215 and get into this young lady's bed. Look as if you lived there. And you two—" She looked at them speculatively for the barest moment, and opened a door that led into a little linen closet. "Get in there and keep quiet."

The plump brunette ran through the door and down the hall with surprising speed and agility. Molly Coppins shoved Jake and Helene into the little linen closet, shut the door, locked it, and withdrew the key.

"Hope she doesn't forget where she hides the key," Jake whispered. He put his arms around Helene and held her close, realized that she was shivering from head to foot, and patted her comfortingly.

They could hear a thunderous knock at the door.

"I'm coming," Molly called crossly.

There was the sound of an opening door, a brief babble of voices in the distance, voices that grew slowly fainter, and then silence for a very long time. They stood waiting in the stuffy darkness, clinging to each other, hardly daring to breathe.

Then there were the voices again, coming to a slow crescendo outside Molly's door and fading once more into a silence disturbed a moment later by the faint wailing of a police siren that was, in its turn, swallowed up by the quiet night. Molly unlocked and opened the door. They stood for a minute blinking at the light.

"It's all over," Molly told them. "They wanted to look in 215 because it was empty when they were here before, and it looked like a woman lived there. It's all right. They won't look there again."

"Why not?" Jake asked, one arm around Helene.

The fat woman chuckled. "Rose peeled off her kimono and was in bed when they knocked. She didn't answer the door and I unlocked it for them. She sat bolt upright in bed, mother naked, and cursed us out for waking her. Boy, did she give those cops an earful!" She chuckled again. "I bet they're blushing yet. They still think their blonde firebug lives in the building, but they won't look in 215 again. You'll be safe there, Miss Brand."

Jake looked at Helene. She was very pale, swaying ever so little. He picked her up like a child.

"Help me get her to bed, Molly. She's all in."

"And no wonder," Molly said sympathetically.

Jake carried her up the stairs; Molly helped her to undress and tucked her in bed. Jake washed the soot from her face and hands, and patted the covers up under her chin. She lay there like an exhausted child.

"Poor little thing," Molly said, adding, "too bad she's so tired. Jake. This would be a wonderful time to get up a party."

Jake looked up at the windows, saw just a faint gray light coming through.

He reached down and patted Helene's cheek, she opened her eyes for a moment and smiled at him.

"You may have forgotten it," he told her, "but this was the night we were going to go to Crown Point and get married!"

"*One* of the nights," said Helene, and was asleep before Jake could answer.

CHAPTER 25

Jake inquired at the hotel desk for John J. Malone, was told that the little lawyer had come in a few hours before and gone up to his room. He looked at his watch, riding up in the elevator, and reflected that this was an ungodly hour to wake anyone. Still, what was the use of having a lawyer if you couldn't wake him up before dawn to get you out of a jam. Especially a jam like this one.

The door to Malone's room was ajar. The lawyer was fast asleep in a chair by the window, a little avalanche of cigarette ashes on his vest. Jake shook him into wakefulness.

"What the hell?" Malone said, blinking, "what the hell? Where did you go? I waited here an hour or so, and then I drove to Erie Street and couldn't find you, so I stopped to watch a fire for a while, and came back here."

"That was our fire," Jake said proudly, "too bad you didn't stick around longer."

He told Malone of the pursuit of Helene.

"Just our luck," he finished, "that damned waitress saw Helene and me around the place."

"What were you doing there, for the love of God?"

"Carrying Paul March's body out, so we could take it up to St. John's house," Jake said, lighting a cigarette and snapping the match toward the wastebasket.

The lawyer bounded to his feet, wide-awake now.

"Jake Justus, you're drunk."

"That may be," Jake agreed, "and it's been said earlier tonight, too, but I know what I'm talking about."

Malone paced the floor a minute or so. "I might have known better than to let you two wander around alone, even for an hour or two. It's God's mercy you didn't think of dynamiting the city hall. Did you really find

Paul March's body, and how did you do it, and where was it, and where is it now?"

"We really did, and it was in the freezing chamber of the old warehouse, and right now it's leaning against the door of John St. John's kitchen."

He added the details of the night's adventures.

Malone stared out the window, biting savagely at a cigar. "It would have been simpler if you'd just gone ahead and gotten married, as you originally intended."

"How was I to know?" Jake asked innocently.

"God only knows what's going to happen now," Malone said gloomily, sinking into a chair. He looked at Jake. "You'd better get some sleep."

"Hell, I can sleep anytime. How are we going to get Helene out of this mess? It's my fault in the first place, and that doesn't make me feel any better about it either."

"For two cents," Malone said irritably, "for two cents I'd drop the whole thing and let you get her out of it yourself."

"Filthy moneygrubber," said Jake admiringly. "What are you going to do, Malone?"

The lawyer sighed deeply. "Oh hell, I'll fix it up. But Helene will have to lie low until I do. The police captain at the Chicago Avenue station is a friend of mine. He knows you two, as you might have remembered. I'll tell him how it happened, and get the whole thing dropped. Now get some sleep."

"What's going to happen when the body is discovered tomorrow? Paul March's body?"

"Hell will pop," Malone said darkly. "I hope to God your pal Essie was able to get away with those letters."

"I hope so too," Jake said. "I should have gone in and made sure, but I was too afraid of waking the guy." He yawned and stretched. "Maybe you're right. Maybe I'd better go home and get some sleep."

"Maybe you'd better stay right where you are," Malone told him. "The police might have a description of the blond pyromaniac's companion. You wouldn't be able to get much sleep in the jailhouse."

Jake said wearily, "I guess not." He walked to the window and looked out. Grant Part was misty and mysterious in the vapors that rolled in from the lake. Like Helene's dress, he thought. Cloud color. Beyond the lake a faint line of rose marked where the sun was going to rise in a few minutes.

"This looks like a good day for getting married," he said. He stretched again and lay down on the bed. "Is there a drink in the house?"

Malone unearthed a bottle of gin from under a pile of shirts, and poured some into a glass. Jake drank it gratefully.

"My God, I'm tired. Malone, you don't think St. John's implication in the Paul March murder is going to involve Nelle, do you?"

"How the hell would I know?" the lawyer growled, pulling off his shirt. "You go to sleep. I'm going to take a shower and get some breakfast and go find out about things."

"Wouldn't it be one hell of a note if St. John hadn't really shot the guy?"

"Wouldn't it," Malone said coldly.

"Well, you can't expect me to think of everything. I don't like St. John anyway. If he didn't do it, let him prove it."

"Shut up and go to sleep."

The lawyer went into the bathroom and slammed the door.

The sound of the shower running made a pleasant accompaniment to Jake's thoughts. Scenes floated before his mind in unordered succession: Helene, the broadcast, the bruise on Essie St. John's shoulder, Helene, the moment when they had crossed the bridge one shuddering second before the barrier fell, lines of dialogue from next week's script, Helene again. He slept.

Hours later he woke, looked around him, tried to remember what had happened and why he was sleeping on Malone's bed with all his clothes on. Something strange, something far from normal, had happened to his head. He wondered what it could have been, and if he would ever feel the same again.

He reached for the telephone, inquired about the time. It was half-past eleven. He laid down the telephone, wondering why he hadn't simply looked at his watch.

One by one the events of the past night came back to his mind. He sat up and swung his long legs to the floor, watched the floor tilt sideways, spin a little, tremble, and settle back to normal. It was a little unnerving. If Malone had any gin left, a drink would either make him feel better or worse.

Ten minutes later he decided that it had made him feel decidedly better.

Again he picked up the telephone, and called Molly Coppins. She reported that Helene was still sleeping soundly and that she would not, under any circumstances, let anyone bother her, including Jake Justus.

He helped himself to Malone's razor, shaved, and took a shower. He was just tying the mildest of Malone's neckties, his own being beyond repair, when the lawyer walked into the room.

"Everything fixed up?" he asked.

"No," the lawyer said sourly. "Everything is in a mess. Perhaps this will be a lesson to you. Perhaps this will teach you to let well enough alone. I doubt it, but I can't help hoping it will."

"Have the police arrested St. John for murder yet?"

"No. And they won't. Not now, or at any future time."

Jake spun around. "Why the hell not?"

"Because St. John is dead," Malone said, tossing a folded newspaper on the dresser. "Because someone shot St. John last night."

"Malone, for the love of God!"

"This morning the St. John maid walked in the back door, knocked over Paul March's body, and was scared out of seven years' growth. In the living room the radio was blatting away with some good-morning-cheer-up program. She rushed into the living room and there sat St. John in front of the radio, a bullet through his bean."

"Malone," Jake said desperately, "Malone, he must have been dead when we were there last night."

He picked up the paper. A smudged and unflattering picture of John St. John adorned the front page.

DOUBLE SLAYING IN
RADIO EXECUTIVE'S HOME

DIRECTOR FOUND
SHOT TO DEATH
BESIDE RADIO SET

Jake glanced hastily through the story. The police, it seemed, were somewhat puzzled by the condition of Paul March's body. He wondered how much it had thawed out before they arrived. The police had likewise fixed the time of the murder at some hour before midnight. This had been decided when it was found that the radio set was turned to a station which went off the air at twelve. Smart of them, he thought.

Another headline caught his eye.

BLOND PYROMANIAC
SOUGHT BY POLICE

"Malone, what have you done about this damned mess Helene is in?"

"Nothing yet. I can't be everywhere at once, and this St. John murder comes first. I'd rather get you out of a murder rap than an arson charge."

Jake remembered something very suddenly. "Malone! The letters. Nelle's letters. Did Essie get them before the murder?"

"Before the murder, or after it, or at the time of it," Malone said. "At least the police didn't find them in his pocket—I was able to learn that much, anyway. So I stopped at your hotel to find out if she'd left them for you, and she hadn't. But I learned that announcer, Bob Bruce, has been trying to reach you since four o'clock this morning. You'd better call him right away."

Jake stared at him. "Bob Bruce? Why does he want to get in touch with me?"

"Probably wants to confess to the murders, and thinks you have a sympathetic face," the lawyer said crossly. "Why don't you call him up and find out?"

Jake picked up the telephone and called Bob Bruce.

"Oh thank God," the announcer said, his smooth, overtrained voice harsh and desperate. "Get over here right away, will you? I can't tell you over the phone. But there's one hell of a jam."

"Wait, Bob. Let me bring Malone with me. Malone, the lawyer. You know him."

"Lord yes. He's just the man we need. But hurry, will you? This is an awful mess!"

CHAPTER 26

Bob bruce's apartment was on the top floor of a building only a few blocks north of Erie Street, overlooking the lake. The handsome young announcer, his face pale with anxiety and loss of sleep, ushered them into a large living room that was a confused horror of modernistic furniture and paintings.

Essie St. John sat near the window on a contortion of chromium-plated gas pipe and pink leather.

"Fancy meeting you here!" Jake said pleasantly.

She had the appearance of one who has been holding back hysteria for unnumbered hours. At the sound of Jake's voice she immediately burst into frantic tears.

"Essie, please, darling, please, Essie," Bob Bruce said, kneeling beside her.

She buried her face in her hands, shaking from head to foot. In a minute, Jake saw, she would begin screaming.

"Bob, where's the bathroom?"

"In there."

Jake soaked a towel in ice water, shoved Essie's head back against his arm, and slapped her gently with the towel until she grew quiet. He could hear Malone out in the kitchen, making noises that indicated coffee was being made.

"Oh Jake," she said weakly. "I'm terribly sorry. I just couldn't help it. I've been trying not to for so long and then all of a sudden you were here and I couldn't help it."

"Don't apologize," he said. "I often have that effect on people." He sponged her face with the towel, lit a cigarette, and held it to her mouth. "You'd better powder your nose."

She managed a faint and unconvincing smile.

"Now take a long breath and tell me what happened," he said very calmly.

"Bob, you tell him. I can't. I can't talk about it."

Bob Bruce wrinkled his good-looking face into an appalling scowl. "Jake, it's a mess. A terrible mess."

"You told me that over the phone, and I'll take your word for it. What happened?"

"Well—last night Essie told me what she was going to do. You know what I mean. We—I—we had a date. Never mind that. Anyway, she told me. About the letters, and how she was going to get them. It's all right— her telling me, I mean. She knew she could trust me."

"Yes, yes, yes, yes," Jake said, "but go on."

"Well, I wasn't going to let her go out there alone. Hardly. So I drove her out there. We went around the back way. Through the window we could see St. John, slumped over in his chair. I waited in my car and Essie went in by the back door."

"Jake," she interrupted in a little wail, "Jake, there wasn't anything in the kitchen. Not anything. I don't understand—"

"Never mind," Jake said hastily, "tell the rest of it."

Malone, standing in the doorway, signaled him to keep his mouth shut. He nodded almost imperceptibly.

"I went into the living room, and Jake—" She stopped.

"Go on, Essie."

"He was dead," she said in a voice like a whispered scream.

Jake lit a cigarette very deliberately, counted five to himself, and said, "He was dead when you got there?"

"Yes. Yes, he was. I ran out to the car and told Bob. Then I thought about the letters. I thought about someone finding them, the police or someone. So I went back."

He stared at her in amazement.

"I went back and—felt in his pocket—in all his pockets, Jake."

"Good God, Essie!" He looked at her admiringly.

"Jake, they weren't there. They weren't anywhere. *Someone took them.*"

There was a long, terrible silence.

"I guess the coffee's done," Malone said at last. He went into the kitchen, returned with cups and the coffee pot, poured out coffee, and passed it around. No one spoke.

"Oh Jake," Essie said frantically, setting down her cup. "Who shot him? Who shot Paul March and how did his body get there? Who took the letters and where are they? What are we going to do? Oh Jake, what are we going to do?"

Jake crushed out his cigarette. "Essie, I don't know who shot who, or why, and I don't know where the letters are. Let Malone and me worry about those things. But if you had courage enough to go back in that room last night, you've got the courage to do what you've got to do now." He thought for a moment. "Will your sister have had sense enough—"

Bob Bruce spoke up. "I phoned her just before you got here. I just said, 'Do you know where Essie is?' She knew what I meant, and she said that Essie had been there all night, and was sleeping. She said no one had tried to locate her out there yet, but that if anyone did, she'd tell them Essie was sleeping."

"Good," Jake said, "evidently the whole family thinks on its feet. Where's your car, Bob?"

"Parked right around the corner, on Pearson Street."

"All right. You drive Essie out to her sister's. Pray that no one gets a look at her on the way. Then get away from there as fast as you can and spend the rest of the day giving the impression you don't know a thing about this. Essie, you and your sister make double sure that alibi of yours is foolproof. And then, by God, you take a sedative and get into bed. Take something that will keep you asleep all day. I don't imagine you had any sleep last night."

She shook her head. "I've just been sitting here by the window, trying to think, and finally all I could think of was for Bob to find you."

"Well, you stay asleep all day. I'll send a doctor friend of mine out to see you late this afternoon, and he'll give you something to make you keep on sleeping, and he'll announce to the police that you're in a state of complete collapse, not fit to be questioned. By the time they do get to question you, either you'll have your nerves in good shape so you can stand up under it, or the murderer will have been found and it won't matter."

"All right, Jake." She drew a long, shuddering breath. "I'll do just as you say."

"Good girl." He patted her shoulder.

Malone spoke up from his post by the doorway. "Jake's advice is good, and be sure you follow it. But, just between ourselves, and just to keep the record clear, did you shoot him?"

She looked up, wide-eyed. "No."

Bob Bruce said angrily, "Of course she didn't."

"Don't mind me," Malone said. "I don't care. I was just curious. But if the whole story comes out, your part of it is going to look fishy as hell."

Essie St. John spoke slowly and deliberately, "No, I didn't shoot him. But so many times I've wished I had nerve enough to do it. Now he's dead and I'm free. I can't believe it."

Bob Bruce knelt beside her again, put an arm around her gently. "You'll believe it in time. The whole thing is going to seem like a nightmare that's all done with. And when it's all over and forgotten, and we're married, perhaps I can make you happy enough to make up for all of it."

"Well, well," Jake said, "what a wonderful time for a proposal."

No one paid any attention to him. Least of all, Essie St. John. She stared at the young announcer. "But Bob. You mean you really want to marry *me?*"

"Of course I do, you nitwit," Bob said almost crossly. "I've been in love with you for weeks—months—hell, I've been in love with you forever."

"But Bob," she said again. "But I'm so—homely!" Tears trembled in her eyes again.

"Don't be such a sap," he said, and this time his voice was really cross. "You're the most beautiful woman I ever saw, and you know it."

Jake could tell that he meant it from the bottom of his heart.

"Very pretty," Malone said, "and for the love of God, get out of here and on your way." His voice was unexpectedly gentle.

Out on the sidewalk, Jake said to Malone. "That reminds me, I'm going to be married myself. Do you think we can make it today?"

"I doubt it," Malone said. "At least, your bride-to-be has to stay hidden out until I get this arson charge off her neck." He sighed. "Arson, body snatching, obstruction of justice, falsifying evidence, and resisting arrest. Resisting an officer in the attempt to do his duty—hell, a whole squad car full of officers."

"Not only that," Jake said, "Helene also drove through a stop light."

"All she has to do now is slap a policeman," the lawyer said gloomily, "and she'll get life."

"Malone, who shot St. John?"

"I don't know, but I hope his wife didn't. That looks like the start of a beautiful romance."

"She said she didn't shoot him," Jake observed. "Don't you believe her?"

"I never believe anybody," Malone said sourly. "I always expect people to lie to me. That's how I always know exactly where I stand."

"Just assuming for the moment that Essie is telling the truth," Jake began.

Malone interrupted him. "By a strange coincidence, at least I hope it's a coincidence, the person who benefits most by the death of Paul March and by the death of Mr. Givvus and now by the death of John St. John is none other than Nelle Brown."

"Malone, you can't think she's guilty of murder."

"Leave what I think out of this. I only hope the police don't think she is."

"Damn it," Jake said crossly, "they can't."

"Who are you to tell what the police can or can't do?" Malone said. "Hope for the best and keep your fingers crossed. And now, for the love of God, let's have breakfast."

CHAPTER 27

They walked to Erie Street, found Helene awake, and while Malone went to the corner delicatessen for breakfast materials, Jake told her all that had been happening. By the time he had finished, it was one in the afternoon, and Malone had breakfast on the table.

"There's a certain austere simplicity about this murderer that I'm beginning to enjoy," the lawyer said, buttering a piece of toast.

"Simplicity!" Helene said indignantly.

"You heard me," Malone said. "There's no nonsense about him. No obscure poisons, no time bombs, no mysterious messages pinned on the wall. He wants somebody out of the way, so he just walks in and shoots him."

"You're right about the simplicity," Jake said. "We're the ones who seem to complicate everything."

"In the case of Paul March," Malone went on, "the murderer came to his apartment, sensibly picked a time when the radio program coming through the loud-speaker would cover the sound of the shot, and shot March neatly through the forehead. Then when he decided to murder Givvus, he went into the client's room at a time when The Rider of the Rockies was filling the air with racket, and tidily shot Mr. Givvus just behind the right ear. And last night, he evidently waited till St. John was alone, calmly walked in the house—"

"There weren't any shot-and-shell programs on the air last night," Helene said. "I looked through the program listings."

"Just the same," Malone told her, "I'd be willing to place a small bet that our murderer picked a good noisy program and turned St. John's loud-speaker on full when he fired the shot. Patterns tend to repeat themselves."

"There's one pattern I hope doesn't go on repeating itself," Jake said gloomily. "Helene and me driving bodies around the streets of Chicago."

"I could mention another," Helene said. "You and me trying to get married."

"Don't be discouraged," Malone said. "I once knew a couple who were engaged for eleven years."

"I never believed in long engagements," Jake said. "Malone, what happened out there last night?"

"I don't know," Malone said, "but three murders, if committed by the same person, ought to be easier to solve than one." He sighed deeply. "The thing that bothers me about these damned murders is that they all benefit Nelle Brown. This glamour-pants Paul March was blackmailing her. Somebody shot him. The guy Givvus was trying to get his hands on her show. Somebody shot him. John St. John had a copy of the Paul March letters and conceivably knew about the Paul March murder. Somebody shot him. The inference," he said, stirring his coffee violently, "is obvious. Too obvious, in fact, for me to credit."

"You mean it looks so much as if she had shot all three of them that you don't think she did?" Helene inquired.

Malone sighed again. "But the only indication of her innocence is that she says she didn't do it."

"That's enough for me," Jake said.

"You aren't a jury," Malone reminded him. "You aren't the public. But assuming it wasn't Nelle, and that protecting her was the motive, who thought enough of her to murder three guys for her?"

"Any God's number of people," Jake said.

"How about Baby?" Malone asked.

"He didn't like Paul March," Jake said slowly, "and he knew about Nelle's affair with Paul. He might have known March was trying to blackmail her. In fact anybody who stole Nelle's script last week might have known it. He had the opportunity. When I called him on the phone that night, he was alone, and his apartment is only a few blocks from here. He could have nipped over here, shot March, and nipped back again. In the case of Givvus—He would have had to know all that St. John was trying to do, to have had any motive for murdering the man. Even then, would he have shot Mr. Givvus just so that St. John couldn't sell him a program?"

"Men have been murdered for less," Malone said.

"He was at the studios," Jake went on. "He says he was taking a nap in the announcer's room. He would have known that The Rider of the Rockies was on, with all its gunfire effects. And last night—" He paused. "Last night, of course, the motive would have been to get Nelle's letters back from St. John, if he knew St. John had them. As far as we know, he had ample opportunity last night." He scowled. "Motive a little weak perhaps, but opportunity one hundred per cent in all three cases."

"Of course," Helene pointed out, "it's still possible that none of these murders had anything to do with Nelle Brown."

"Possible but improbable," Malone said, "and it's been my experience that while impossible things happen frequently, improbable ones never do."

Jake was paying no attention. "You can take the name of almost anyone on the show," he said slowly, "and apply the motive of getting Nelle out of a nasty jam."

"Even going as far as murder?" Helene asked incredulously.

"As far and even farther," Jake told her. "There isn't a person on the show who doesn't damn near worship Nelle. In the first place, no one can help liking her, you know that yourself, of course. But it's more than that. There isn't one person on that show Nelle hasn't done some very swell thing for.

"Baby, of course, is crazy about her," he went on. "Oscar—he got in a very bad way a year or so ago; Nelle sent him through an alcoholic cure, lent him money, got him back on his feet again. Lou Silver—Nelle got him out of an unpleasant blackmailish jam with a dame. Bob Bruce was practically on his uppers and couldn't get a job to save his life, when Nelle fought, bled, and all but died to get him on her show. She straightened out a hellish mess between McIvers and his wife. When Schultz's kid was in the hospital with a serious operation, Nelle put up the money. There's other stuff I could tell you, and probably a lot more I don't know about. Add that to the person Nelle is. See? When she smashed up over Paul March last winter, everybody on the show suffered damn near as much as she did. Commit murder for her? Hell's bells, any one of that crew would *be* murdered for her."

"A beautiful speech," Malone said. "It does you credit, and what's more, I believe it. But it doesn't tell me who murdered who." He paused to mop his face with a soiled and crumpled handkerchief. "What's more, I'd like to know how much goofier Tootz is than we think he is."

They stared at him for a full minute.

"Oh Malone," Helene said, "you couldn't imagine Tootz being a homicidal maniac."

"Understand this," Malone said, frowning, "you think of a homicidal maniac as a wild creature with tangled hair and flaming eyes, foaming at the mouth, and brandishing an ax. That isn't the right picture at all. A crazy man can be crafty as hell. He can fool a lot of people."

"But why would he pick on those particular victims?" Jake asked.

"In his condition of mind, he might pick on anybody," Malone said. "Delusions of persecution can bring on a bunch of murders. Especially if he thought those particular people were persecuting Nelle."

"But that's why it's impossible," Jake said. "He didn't know anything about them. Not about Paul March, nor Givvus—hell, he didn't know Givvus from a circus horse. He didn't know anything about anything." He scowled ferociously. "Damn it, Malone, half of our anxiety is over keeping Tootz from finding out about any of this."

"There's another reason why it's impossible," Helene said thoughtfully. "Tootz couldn't have been there."

"Helene's right," Jake said. "All his horses couldn't drag Tootz out of the house when Nelle wasn't with him. And in the case of all three of the murders, Nelle was away from Tootz."

Malone shrugged his shoulders. "Well anyway, that would still leave a long list of questions unanswered." He checked on his fingers. "One, what was the motive for moving Paul March's body? Two, where did March get the money that was in his pocket? Three, who stole Nelle Brown's script with the impression of the blackmail note on it? Four, where are the letters St. John was carrying in his pocket yesterday? Five, who set fire to the old warehouse?"

Jake blinked.

"After all," Malone added, "it doesn't seem likely that the warehouse would have chosen this particular time to burn down, just all by itself."

There was a long, uncomfortable pause.

"And to think," Jake said at last, "all this started with one measly little murder that nobody cared about, and that I thought nobody would ever know anything about. Personally," he muttered, "I think it's a conspiracy just to keep me from getting married to Helene. Somebody's doing the whole thing just to make life hard for me."

"Von Flanagan is probably thinking the same thing right now," Malone said. "He thinks murderers try to hide the evidences of their crimes as a personal unkindness to him."

"Would it do any good," Jake said slowly, "for me to go to Van Flanagan and tell him my part in the whole mess? Leaving out the part about the letters, of course. But if he knew about the secret audition, and where Givvus was killed, and where March was killed and when—"

"It might have done some good if you'd thought of it earlier," Malone said. "Von Flanagan is too sore about it now. He'd love an excuse to throw anybody in the jug right now, and you've given him plenty of reason for arresting you. You'd better not stick your neck out any more than it is already, or Von Flanagan will have a noose around it."

Jake said, "No noose is good noose," and blushed apologetically.

"I'll tell you what you can do," Malone told him. "I'm going to drop in at Von Flanagan's office and you can come along. You have the excuse that your client was associated in a business way with St. John and you want to find out just what is what. But keep your mouth shut and let me do the talking."

Jake nodded.

"And then," Malone continued, "you and I had better go talk to Nelle." He looked at his watch. "The day's practically gone. We'd better get going."

"But what about me?" Helene wailed. "Do I have to stay hidden here forever?"

"I feel a lot safer when you can't roam around and stir up more trouble," Malone said severely. "But I'll do what I can, as soon as I can."

"And meantime, you just stay right where you are," Jake told her.

"All right. I will," she said so meekly that Jake worried about it all the way downtown.

Von Flanagan, when they found him, was not in an amiable mood. He was standing by his window, gloomily watching the traffic in the street below and whistling a bar of "The Last Round-Up," as Jake and Malone walked in.

"You remember Jake Justus," Malone said. "He used to be with the *Examiner*."

Von Flanagan nodded with no warmth whatsoever.

"He's something of a mink fancier himself," Malone added.

The police officer's eyes brightened. "You keep mink?" he asked interestedly.

"Only as pets," Jake said.

"You seem to have quite an affair on your hands," Malone said hastily.

For several minutes Von Flanagan talked loudly and profanely about the murders.

"It's certainly all of that," Malone agreed as the police officer paused for breath. "Jake here is interested because his client—he's a press agent now—was associated with St. John."

Von Flanagan turned to Jake. "Who's your client?"

"Nelle Brown."

"You don't say!" the big man said more cheerfully. "Do you suppose you could get me her autograph?"

"Sure," Jake said, "any time. Who killed John St. John, or do you know yet?"

"Well, his wife might have," Von Flanagan said, "he wasn't any too good to her from what I learn. Only it don't look like she did. Her alibi looks pretty good and anyway she didn't have no reason for shooting the other one."

"The other one?" Malone inquired.

Von Flanagan nodded. "This St. John fella and the guy that was in the kitchen were shot with the same gun. There, by God, we know something, anyway. And we know something else, too. The Paul March guy, he wasn't shot up in St. John's kitchen, he was shot someplace else and took there, just like that other bird, Givvus, was took up to Lincoln Park. It would look like the same thing, only the Givvus murder don't seem to have nothing to do with these two, on account of he was shot with a different gun. But this here Paul March, I don't know where he was shot, and God only knows when he was shot, because there's something funny about the condition of his body. But wherever he was shot, he was took up to where we found him."

"That's curious," Jake said weakly. It was the best he could do at the time."

"What's more," Von Flanagan said, "now it looks like there was some tie-up between these murders and this guy Givvus. On account of the one thing we did find out about this guy Givvus is that he'd sent a bunch of money to Paul March just a few days before he came to Chicago." He leaned back precariously in his chair and folded his hands across his middle.

Malone considered the end of his cigar very thoughtfully and said, "What do you suppose he did that for?"

"Search me," the police officer said, "I'm no crystal-gazer. All I know is this guy Givvus sent this guy Paul March a check for five hundred bucks, with a voucher attached reading, 'For services rendered.' I know that, and I know three guys are dead, and I know the papers are raising hell with me. And I don't like it."

"I don't blame you," Malone said soothingly.

"Somebody moved those two bodies," Von Flanagan said, an indignant light coming into his eyes, as though he considered it a grave personal affront. "Somebody did, and me, I ain't gonna stand for it. I don't know who done it, but I'm sure as shooting going to find out. And boy," he said gleefully, rubbing his hands together, "boy, when I *do* get my hands on whoever it was—"

CHAPTER 28

"Well, we didn't learn much from Von Flanagan," Malone said on the way to Nelle's apartment. "Just that Mr. Givvus sent Paul March five hundred bucks, and that if Von Flanagan ever lays hands on you, God help you."

"Damn it," Jake said indignantly, "I wasn't the first person to move Paul March's mortal remains. Somebody else started this juggling process. Malone, why did Givvus send the money to March?"

"You're as good a guess artist as I am," Malone said noncommittally. "Offhand I can think of several dozen reasons, and none of them seem in the least reasonable."

"Malone, you've got to do something!"

"I am going to do something," the little lawyer said.

"What?"

"I'm going to move to Australia," Malone said sourly, "and raise mink."

They found Nelle in the big, paneled living room, talking animatedly to a tall, slender girl. The girl had bobbed black hair, wore eyeglasses attached to a wide ribbon, and was dressed austerely in a gray tailored suit.

"Hello," Nelle said happily, "I'm so glad you finally got here." She didn't bother to introduce the black-haired girl. "I've just been telling the story to this young lady from the *Times*."

"You've been doing what?" Jake asked in a dazed voice.

"It's very interesting that she was really the one to find Paul March's body," the young woman said. Her speech was high-pitched and affected. Jake disliked her at the first sound of it.

"My God, Nelle!"

Nelle looked at him with wide, hurt eyes. "Oh Jake! Did I do wrong?"

Jake groaned. "Damn it, Nelle, you know I never want you to talk to reporters. You know I handle all these things myself. And now—" The implications of what she had done grew in his mind with a mounting horror. "After I've practically broken my neck, risked a jail sentence, and God knows what else besides, just to keep you out of the newspapers, you go and pull a fool stunt like this and ruin everything—" He stopped and wondered what the hell Nelle was laughing about.

"This will teach you to label me a pyromaniac," the young woman said in Helene's voice.

Jake looked at her, at the black, bobbed wig, the eye-glasses, the tailored suit. Probably for the first time in his life, he was speechless.

"Well after all," Helene said, "you couldn't expect me to sit around with my hands folded."

"Where in the name of God did you get the wig?" Jake said. His voice hadn't quite recovered.

"Molly borrowed it from a girl who works in a burlesque show. The nice young man next door went to the dimestore and got the glasses for me. The suit belongs to a model who lives on the floor above. Who is going to be arrested for St. John's murder?"

Nelle looked up, her face suddenly grave, "Yes, Jake. Tell it all quick before Tootz gets through being shaved and comes in here."

Jake told them what little they had learned from Von Flanagan.

"Nelle, where were you last night?" Malone asked.

"But I didn't kill him—"

"I never said you did. I want to know what kind of an alibi you've got."

"I went to see Baby. Bigges drove me there and went off someplace and then came back and got me. I got home a little after midnight."

"A wonderful alibi," Jake said sourly. "It'll look nice in print, too."

"All right," she said irritably, "I had a headache and couldn't sleep so Bigges took me for a drive and brought me home again."

"That's weak, but it sounds better."

"Jake, the police don't suspect me, do they?"

"I don't think so," he told her, "but you're bound to be questioned. You get this into your head and keep it there. One, you only knew St. John in a business way. Two, you haven't any idea who might have wanted to murder him. Three, you were riding around with Bigges last night."

"But Jake. The copies of my letters. Where are they?"

"I wish to God I knew," Jake said soulfully.

"Find the murderer and you'll find the letters," Helene said. "They were in St. John's pocket yesterday afternoon."

"Oh Jake," Nelle said desperately, "Tootz mustn't know about any of this. Or Baby. But especially Tootz. If either one of them should find out, I'd drop dead."

"Or if Goldman or your public find out, we'll all drop dead," Jake said gloomily, lighting a cigarette.

They heard a door close somewhere in the apartment.

"Here comes Tootz," Nelle whispered.

The handsome, white-haired man walked in, greeted them. He looked a little uncertainly at Helene.

"You know me," Helene said. "I'm me."

He stared at her. "But you've done something to your hair."

"It's a wig," Helene said.

Malone said, "She's disguised."

Tootz smiled and nodded as though that explained everything. "Oh, I see. It's a very good disguise."

"It has to be," Helene said, "I'm being followed. Jake and I were followed everywhere last night, and I thought we'd never get away, so today I disguised myself."

Tootz looked around wonderingly, finally caught Jake's eye, surreptitiously tapped his forehead, glancing at Helene. Jake nodded slowly, almost imperceptibly. Tootz' mouth formed a round O.

"Some of these cases are terribly sad," he murmured softly to Malone.

"Sad," Malone said with feeling, "is hardly a strong enough word for it."

Tootz glanced at the newspaper on the table beside him. "I suppose you've read all about the murders," he said.

Jake cleared his throat. "Yes. We were just talking about it when you came in."

"A horrible thing," Tootz said fastidiously. "I suppose you all knew St. John. I can't say I liked the man, but it's a terrible way to die. It seems to me the other name—March—sounds familiar, but I can't quite place him."

"He was an actor and director," Jake said lamely. "I didn't know him very well myself."

"Neither did I," Nelle managed.

"It seems to me I'd met him," Tootz said, pondering. "I know I did." He drew his brows together and was silent a moment. "Oh yes, I remember now. It was at a party. Nearly a year ago. Remember, Nelle? He seemed rather charming. Too bad this happened."

Malone had been studying a chess problem on the board by the window, he chose that moment to ask Tootz' opinion of it. Tootz slipped into the chair by the chessboard. It was a difficult and involved problem, and the two men discussed it at great length.

"I'm glad you dropped in," Henry Gibson Gifford said happily. "I was getting lonely." He sighed. "It's a fine day out. I wish I dared go walking. But Nelle hasn't wanted to go with me."

"You know," Malone said thoughtfully, studying a chessman, "I've been thinking about those men following you. I think something ought to be done about them."

Tootz nodded gravely. "Something should. But what could be done? Perhaps the police could help."

"I don't think the police would do much good," Malone said. "They're so stupid about things like this. Perhaps I could, though. I've had a lot of experience in one way or another."

A light came into Tootz' eyes. "Do you think you could?"

"Well," Malone said, "I could try. Have you ever thought of doing anything yourself?"

"What?" Tootz asked helplessly.

"For instance," Malone leaned over the table and said very confidentially, "have you ever thought of shooting them?"

Henry Gibson Gifford stared at him, a puzzled look in his fine gray eyes. "But that would be murder."

"Yes," Malone said reflectively, "yes, it would. But it would be justified as self-protection. Or you could shoot at them, and frighten them away."

"I could, couldn't I!" It was as though a sudden ray of hope had crossed the handsome old face. "I could do that. And if they didn't pay any attention, then I would have to really shoot. I hate to think of it, but I could."

"It's a suggestion, anyway," Malone said, picking up a chessman and putting it down again.

"Only—" Henry Gibson Gifford paused, frowned. "I haven't any gun. I'd have to get one. Yes, I'd have to get one. I must speak to Bigges about it." He smiled at the little lawyer. "Thank you very much for your advice, Mr. Malone. I appreciate it greatly."

Conversation went back to the chess problem. At last Malone signaled to Jake that he was ready to leave, and they rose to go, taking Helene with them. At the door, Jake managed one last warning to Nelle, to sit tight and say nothing.

"I wish I had my car," Helene grumbled as they hailed a taxi. "Malone, are you going to get me out of this mess, or aren't you?"

He looked at his watch. "I'll do it now. Andy will be at the police station. In fact, I'll even take you with me, wig and all."

"Wonderful," Helene said. "I ought to marry you instead of Jake."

"While I'm doing it," the lawyer went on, "why don't you, Jake, go have a talk with Baby? He'll probably be freer with you than with me. Find out if there's anything he knows that we don't know."

Jake scowled. "I hope he doesn't."

"So do I, but we're leaving no turn unstoned."

"That's wrong," Helene said. "It's that we're leaving no worm unturned. Malone, is Tootz a homicidal maniac?"

Malone said, "Hell no. And in any case, I can only see these murders being committed by a sane man."

Jake left them in front of the remodeled mansion where Baby lived, promising to meet them at the corner bar in half an hour.

Baby was in, looking very pale and very tired. Jake wondered if he had gotten any sleep the night before. In fact, he wondered if anybody had gotten any sleep the night before. Except, of course, John St. John. The young man seemed almost terribly glad to see him.

"Jake," he said, "I need your advice. Do you think I ought to go to the police and confess to these murders?"

Jake dropped the cigarette he was in the act of lighting, picked it up again, and finished lighting it before he spoke.

"Is that your idea of fun," he said, "or did you do them?"

"No," Baby said. "But eventually the police will find out who really did, and it'll be all right. And in the meantime, it will help Nelle."

"You aren't real," Jake said. "People like you don't happen. You've been reading the wrong kind of magazines. Look here, kid, suppose Nelle herself is really guilty?"

"But she isn't. I knew she couldn't be when I read in the papers that both St. John and Paul March were shot with the same gun. I knew she didn't shoot St. John because she was here last night. So, of course, she couldn't have done the other. She couldn't have anyway. Not Nelle. I should have known—" His voice broke off suddenly.

"What should you have known?" Jake asked.

The young man buried his face in his hands. "I've been an awful fool. All this time I've been thinking Nelle killed Paul March, and then Mr. Givvus, and I've been nearly going crazy."

Jake stared at him. "But nobody knew about Paul March's murder until this morning."

"I did," Baby said miserably. "I knew it all along." He looked up, his face strained and white. "Jake, that night—the night of the broadcast—I'd been over at a friend's apartment listening to the show, because my radio was on the fritz. It was over and I was just walking home along Erie Street, when I saw Nelle get out of a taxi in front of the building there."

"Did she see you?" Jake asked.

Baby shook his head. "I started to call to her, and then I stopped. I knew she was going to see Paul March. Or I supposed she was. I wasn't sure. I waited there for her to come out. This all sounds crazy, but you do crazy things when you're as jealous as I was that night. Finally she did come out, and went away. I was nearly wild, wondering if she'd been to see him. I thought I'd just go in and see if he was there. I thought that if he was there, then I'd feel sure she'd been to see him. So I walked up to his door. It was just a little open and I—went in. Oh hell, I don't know what I thought I'd say to him or do to him. I just went in. And there he was, dead." He looked up at some indeterminate point on the ceiling. "I supposed Nelle had shot him."

Jake walked to the window, watched two taxicabs and a truck roll down the street, turned back again. "Good God," he said, and again, "good God! And you've been carrying this around on your back all this time!"

"I couldn't say anything to her, could I? I couldn't do anything, could I? I just had to keep still. And then the day of the audition—" He paused.

"Go on," Jake said.

"I knew the secret audition was going on. And I was just coming out of Studio B and I saw Givvus going into the client's room with St. John. And I just sort of figured it out myself—that St. John was making Nelle give the audition. I knew she wouldn't want to do such an audition. I wasn't sure how St. John was making her do it, but I knew he must be. And then I read in the paper that Givvus had been killed."

"And you thought Nelle killed him!" Jake said.

"What could I think?" The young man said wildly. "What could I think? I know now I was wrong, but still that doesn't help much. My God, Jake, what am I going to do? I can't just not do anything at all about it."

"All you can do is keep your mouth shut, and be nice to Nelle," Jake told him. "She's having it tough right now. Are you in tomorrow night's show?"

"Yes. Oscar called me this morning."

"Good. Just stick around and—well, be nice to her. That's all you can do."

"I know she doesn't love me," Baby said, "but that doesn't make any difference. I'd do anything. Anything, Jake."

"No, she doesn't love you," Jake said gently, "and she never will. She's in love with a dream, and she always will be. Right now the dream happens to look like you. She means every word she says to you now. But someday the dream will change and look like somebody else. Maybe we all love only imaginary people, I don't know. But certainly Nelle does. And when the change does come, you're the one it'll be tough on."

"No it won't," the young man said. "I can remember her, can't I?"

Jake shook his head pityingly.

"You think I'll get over it," Baby said, "but I won't."

"You'll remember her," Jake said, getting up. "But your own dream will change. Hell, what are we looking into the future for? The present is bad enough." He sighed. "The truth is, the only person Nelle really loves is Tootz, strange as it seems." He paused at the door. "Keep your mouth shut and try not to worry."

Baby nodded. "I will."

Down on the sidewalk, Jake glanced at his watch. There would be time to walk over to his hotel and change his clothes before he met Malone and Helene again. Not, he told himself, that he was getting dressed to get married. To think that would be to tempt providence. But sleeping in his clothes had not improved them any.

Something had to be done about Baby. In the past, Nelle's romances hadn't bothered him. This wouldn't as far as Nelle herself was concerned. But sooner or later the young man was in for a blow. A bad blow. Perhaps if he talked firmly to Nelle, she'd ease Baby down and end the whole affair. Nelle wouldn't want to hurt anybody if she could help it. Or perhaps he could convince Baby that his presence on the scene was harmful to Nelle and get him to go away. It had to be ended somehow.

Hell's bells, why was he wasting his time over it? As if he didn't have enough on his mind anyway. Perhaps by this time Malone was getting Helene squared with the police. They would meet for dinner in a little while now, and he would be able to forget Nelle, Baby, the police, the murders, and everything else for a few hours.

He walked into the lobby of his hotel. A tall, gangling young man rose from a chair near the door and came to meet him.

"Thank God you got here," Joe McIvers said. "I've been going nuts!"

CHAPTER 29

"You're damned right. I'm not glad to see you," Jake said crossly, ushering McIvers into his room and kicking the door shut. "Last Sunday I started

out to get married. This is Thursday night and, between one cursed murder and another, I haven't got around to it yet."

He lighted a cigarette and stared at McIvers. "How about a drink?"

"Thanks," McIvers said. "I guess I could use one."

"You look it," Jake grunted. He dug the remains of a bottle of gin out of
a dresser drawer and divided it with mathematical precision into two
glasses. "I'm meeting my girl and my lawyer in just twenty-one minutes
and possibly by the grace of God we'll be able to get married tonight."

"Does it take a lawyer to get you married?" McIvers asked a little stupidly.

"No," Jake said, "he's just getting my girl out of jail." He pulled off his
shirt and began searching for a clean one.

"But Jake," the agency man said unhappily, "everything is in such a
mess."

"That statement has no news value whatsoever," Jake told him. He looked
at McIvers closely. "Something's on your mind. You might as well tell me
and get it over with."

"It's about Paul March's murder," McIvers said. "You see, I was there."

An act of providence saved Jake from dropping the glass of gin.

"I was there," the agency man repeated. "And about the warehouse, you
know. There's a newspaper story about its burning down. If it burned
down Paul March's body should have been burned up in the fire, only
how could it have been there if it was in St. John's kitchen, and anyway,
how did it get there?"

Jake sat down on the edge of the bed and stared at him.

"It gets sort of complicated," McIvers said.

"Let's start this all over again," Jake said very slowly and calmly. "How
did you know Paul March's body was in the warehouse?"

"God damn it," the agency man said wildly, "I put it there."

"Well, well," Jake said after a while. He began changing his socks. "You
didn't shoot him, by any chance?"

"No. No, I didn't. He was dead when I got there. Jake, you've got to
believe me."

"Sure," Jake said, "I believe you. I've formed a society for believing
people who say they didn't shoot Paul March. But his murder seems to
have been one of the major social events of the season. Hell's bells, everybody was there." He paused and added, "In fact, I was there myself."

"It was because of the script," McIvers said miserably. "I know I shouldn't
have done it, but what else could I do?"

Jake gave up all attempts at dressing, and said, "Getting information out of you is like getting an eyewitness story out of a disaster survivor. Do you want to tell me what happened, or do I have to hypnotize you to get it out?"

McIvers frowned. "It's sort of complicated."

"You said that before," Jake reminded him. "What's this about the script and what did you do that you shouldn't have done because there was nothing else to do?"

"Nelle had written some letters to Paul March," McIvers said, "and he was threatening to send them to Goldman, so I moved the body."

Jake looked at him for fifteen seconds, picked up the telephone, and told room service to send up more gin, and said, "Any more of this and I'll land in the paper-doll department, cutting up. You moved Paul March's body?"

"Of course," McIvers said. "What else could I do? It's not just that I like Nelle. Have you any idea how much commission I make off that show?"

"Sure, sure, sure," Jake said. "Go on."

"Nelle's script," McIvers said. "Just before the show I got to looking through it to see about a change that should have been made. And look, Jake, here's how I figure what happened. She must have stuck the note between the pages of the script and it was written in pencil and the pencil came off on the script paper. It was in reverse, but I could read it."

Before Jake had time to wrestle with that, the gin arrived. "So it was you stole the script?" he said, unwrapping the bottle.

"I was afraid someone else would find it," McIvers said. He took the glass Jake handed him. "Thanks for the gin. And then I was afraid Nelle would go over there between broadcasts and I got to worrying, so I went over to Paul March's apartment and he was dead." He paused long enough to gulp the gin. "Jake, why did she do it?"

"Maybe she didn't," Jake said. "But go on. You found him dead, and you did what?"

"I supposed of course she'd shot him. And I had no idea how many people might know she'd gone to his apartment between shows. Or how many people might know about the blackmail note. Or anything. And my God, Jake, imagine what would happen if Nelle was arrested for murder."

Jake said, "I've been imagining it for several days. So you moved the body, huh?"

McIvers jumped up and began pacing the floor. "Damn it, Jake, I had to do something. There was the program to consider. It's the major part of my income. The contract was up for signing again. And anyway, there was Nelle. Suppose—" He paused, gulped. "Good God, suppose poor

Tootz heard anything about it! It would drive him crazy!" He paused and turned pale. "I mean—"

"Never mind," Jake said. "I know what you mean."

"I moved the body," McIvers said. "I remembered the warehouse and the refrigerating chamber. It seemed like a perfect place. I drove my car around to the alley and carried Paul March down the stairs and out the back way, and went up and washed the kitchen floor, and took his body to the warehouse. It was locked, of course, but I didn't have any trouble getting in. Then I went back to the rebroadcast, but I was late, and I just caught the tag end of it out in the lobby. Nelle sounded all right." He stopped and stared at Jake. "You're sure she didn't shoot him?"

"Well," Jake said, "she says she didn't."

McIvers nodded as though that settled everything. "Then the next day I began worrying about it. I was afraid March's disappearance would make some stink. So I sent a note to his landlady with some dough, asking her to send his things to him at Honolulu, and signed his name."

"Why Honolulu?" Jake asked.

"It was the farthest away place I could think of."

"Australia's farther," Jake said. "But that might have been overdoing it."

"But," McIvers said anxiously, "somebody must have discovered the body and taken it up to St. John's kitchen."

"Yes," Jake agreed, "somebody must have."

"It was a crazy thing to do."

"All of that," Jake said with feeling. "But now what?"

"Now Goldman wants to see both of us—you and me—at nine o'clock tomorrow morning," McIvers said anxiously. "Everything was rosy when we came back from Brule. We had a wonderful time fishing, and made all the plans for signing the contract after the show. And then all of a sudden he wants to see both of us tomorrow morning."

"Probably doesn't mean a damn thing," Jake said, buttoning his shirt. "You're just a little haywire because of what's happened, that's all."

"If he had the faintest notion Nelle was involved in the murders, he wouldn't sign."

"He doesn't have any such notion. He can't have. And forget it."

"But if the police are looking for her," McIvers began desperately.

Jake spun around. "What are you talking about?"

"The police," McIvers repeated. "Haven't you seen the papers?"

"Not since morning."

McIvers drew a folded paper from his pocket, Jake grabbed it.

WHO WAS BLOND GIRL
IN RADIO ACTOR'S LIFE?

He read the story hastily. The police had learned of a mysterious and re-
putedly beautiful blond woman who had visited Paul March frequently
during the winter. It was hinted that she might have more to do with his
murder than met the eye. No clue to her identity had been disclosed, but
Von Flanagan had stated he had a good idea who she was, and that he
would have her brought in for questioning before the day was through.

"It means Nelle," McIvers said in a tone that indicated it also meant
ruin.

"Why the hell didn't you tell me this at the beginning?"

"I didn't think of it," the agency man said miserably.

Jake tied his tie with a savage jerk, muttered that he hoped he might be
married by Christmas, and said, "For the love of God, Joe, keep your
mouth shut about all of this. No matter what happens and no matter what
is said, deny everything. Leave Nelle to me, leave the police to Malone,
and leave the rest to God."

"But if it is Nelle," McIvers said, "if it is, and if they do pick her up for
questioning, and if Goldman does hear about it, and if—"

"If all that happens," Jake said, reaching for his hat, "then we'll all go to
Australia and raise mink."

CHAPTER 30

Malone and Helene were waiting for him. She was still wearing the black
wig. It was now slightly askew.

"Your wig is a little woppijawed," he told her. Adding, "So Malone
couldn't get it fixed up for you?"

"He got it fixed up all right," she said. "I've even got the car back. But
I've grown so attached to this wig that I won't give it up."

"All right," he said. "But I'm damned if I'll marry you while you've got
it on. I have a feeling it wouldn't be legal."

He told them McIvers' story on the way to the Erie Street building.
Malone listened silently.

"I have a feeling just like Von Flanagan," he grunted at last. "All this is
being done just to make life hard for me. So McIvers moved Paul March's
body to the warehouse. Then who burned down the warehouse?"

"The man or woman who murdered Paul March," Jake said.

"How did he or she know Paul March's body had been moved to the warehouse?" Malone asked.

After a long pause Helene said, "The murderer's maternal grandmother was a Welshwoman, and he or she has second sight."

Molly Coppins was waiting for them in the lobby. "Jake, the building has been full of policemen all afternoon."

Jake nodded. "I know."

"It's about Paul March, poor devil." She sighed. "To think of my packing all his things and sending them to Honolulu, and all the time he was lying somewhere, dead. Who killed him, Jake?"

"I don't know," Jake said.

Malone sat down on a corner of the desk. "What did they want to know about him—the police, I mean?"

"Oh, everything. Who his friends were, and what he did, and all about him. I didn't know much to tell. He was a sort of unsociable cuss, always kept a little to himself. I don't like people to be like that." She beamed affectionately at Helene.

Helene sighed and said, "Well, I'm glad they've stopped looking for me, anyway."

They went upstairs to Helene's apartment. Jake looked at his watch.

"If we left now," he began, "there ought to be just enough time to drive to—"

"Don't say it!" Helene begged. "I have a feeling that the minute you mention Crown Point, hell will pop somewhere else." She laid the wig on the table, shook out her long, straw-colored hair, and began combing it.

Malone had pulled a crumpled envelope from his pocket and was drawing squares and triangles in the corners.

"Jake," he began slowly, "the Nelle Brown Revue came off the air at nine o'clock—right? And the rebroadcast went on the air at eleven?"

"Right both times," Jake said promptly.

"In between broadcasts—" The lawyer paused, scowled. "Nelle left the studios right after the broadcast. She would have had time to get there while the shot-and-shell program was going on. But we'll assume for the time being that March was already dead when she arrived. In that case, she must have just missed meeting the murderer on his way out."

"And just missed meeting Baby on his way in," Jake said.

"Then," Malone said, "you horsed around trying to figure out where Nelle was, and finally ended up here. After looking the situation over, you beat it back to the studio, with only a few minutes before the rebroadcast.

Meanwhile McIvers thought things over, and was the next arrival on the scene. Did McIvers get back to the rebroadcast?"

"No," Jake said.

Malone scowled at the notes he had made on the envelope, finally crumpled it up, and threw it into a corner. "It all fits in two hours," he announced. "But why did McIvers take so long to get over here?"

"I can tell you that one," Jake said. "The first thing Joe did after the broadcast was to go phone Goldman, the sponsor. Knowing Goldman, I'd say that probably took some time. And Joe's anxiety over what Goldman had thought of the show would keep his mind pretty well occupied for a spell. That happens every week. After he'd phoned Goldman and settled back to normal again, he began to worry about Nelle Brown and the blackmail note, and eventually got over here."

Malone nodded. "Givvus sent five hundred bucks to Paul March," he said thoughtfully. "Paul March was murdered by persons unknown. McIvers played boy scout and moved the remains. Givvus came here for an audition and somebody shot him. Finally, St. John was killed—with the same gun that killed Paul March, but not the gun that killed Givvus."

Jake picked it up from there. "If St. John and Paul March were shot with the same gun, I'd hazard a guess that St. John didn't kill Paul March. There was more than five hundred bucks in Paul March's pants. So possibly St. John bought the Nelle Brown letters from Paul March."

"And where are they now?" Malone asked. "Who wanted them enough to murder St. John for them?"

"You're asking the questions," Jake said. "You can answer them."

"One more question," Malone said. "Do we want to find the murderer?"

"What do you mean?" Jake asked angrily. "If we don't find him, how are we going to get the letters back and get Nelle Brown out of this mess?"

"The problem is this," Malone said. "Suppose the murderer is someone we don't want to find. Grant that St. John is well out of the way. Grant that Paul March is, too. Mr. Givvus seems to have been a perfect nonentity, no one mourns him. How far do you want to go to get Nelle Brown out of a mess?"

"You mean," Jake said, "the murderer may be someone we sympathize with, someone who was perfectly justified in killing."

Malone didn't answer.

"But Malone," Helene said, "murder isn't ever justified."

"Isn't it?" the lawyer said very quietly.

No one answered for a long time.

"The point is this," Malone said at last, "if it's possible to sit tight and do nothing—devote ourselves to making sure that Nelle's place in this picture doesn't become known either by Tootz or Goldman or by the general public—then that's the course of action. Eventually someone else will be murdered somewhere and somehow, and everyone will forget this, maybe even Von Flanagan."

He was interrupted by the door opening suddenly. They turned, and saw Nelle Brown standing in the doorway, big-eyed, breathless, and very pale.

"Jake," she said, her voice strangely flat. "Jake, the police."

Malone bounded up, shut the door, and led her to a chair.

"They came up to the apartment," Nelle went on. "Lucky Tootz didn't hear. Bigges went to the door and they said who they were. Bigges heard me duck in my room and he thought quick and said they'd find me at the studio. So they asked him a lot of questions and went away. But they'll find out I'm not at the studio and go back. Oh Jake, what shall I do?"

"You dad-ratted idiot," Jake said indignantly, "you should have stayed there and let them question you."

"I couldn't, Jake. I'd seen the papers. I know they think I'm—I'm the blonde woman. Oh Jake, between having the show to do tomorrow night, and the script for it doesn't look very good either, and the contract to be signed, and now all this mess, I'm almost crazy. I couldn't stand their asking me a lot of questions now. And suppose they took me somewhere for questioning and the newspapers got hold of it—"

"It wouldn't look so hot," Jake said slowly. "Nelle Brown picked up by police for questioning in Paul March and St. John murders—no, it wouldn't look so hot."

"And Goldman would know, and he wouldn't sign the contract," she said desperately, "and Tootz—"

"What's Tootz going to think if the police go back to your apartment looking for you?" Jake said. "What if they go in and ask him a lot of questions?"

"They won't," Nelle said. "I thought of that. He was restless and not feeling very well anyway, so before I left, Bigges put him to bed and gave him a sedative that'll keep him asleep for hours. If the police go back there, they won't be able to wake him up."

"I want to see that contract signed tomorrow night," Jake said very thoughtfully. "I have a hunch that once it's signed, we'll be safer. If the story does get to Goldman after that, he probably won't do a thing. Not only will Nelle be a valuable property but he'll feel it necessary to protect the show's reputation. So the thing to do is to keep the police from catching up with Nelle until after the contract is signed."

"Very nice," Malone said, "but how? They're probably out looking for her right now."

At that minute there was a knock on the door.

"If it's the police," Jake said, "we give up."

It was not the police. It was the young man from next door, offering beer. Helene welcomed him and told him to close the door. The young man stared suddenly at Nelle.

"I hope I haven't gotten you into any trouble," he said slowly.

"Was it you?" Nelle asked. "Was it you told the police that I'd come here to see Paul March?"

The young man looked unhappy. "It was. I didn't realize I was doing any harm. I didn't tell them your name, but I told them you were pretty and a blonde."

Jake thought fast. "They'd probably discovered Paul March used to be with Nelle's show, and had been seen at parties here and there with Nelle, and when this dope here said 'pretty blonde' they immediately said, 'Ah, Nelle Brown.' "

"I am a dope," the young man said, "and I'm terribly sorry. If there's anything I can do now—"

"Sit down," Helene said absent-mindedly, "and shut up. I'm thinking." She poured out the beer.

"The hell of it is," Jake said, "they'll probably come here, too. Because when they can't find Nelle, they'll naturally look for me to see if I know where she is, and when I left the hotel tonight, I left a message that I'd be here in case anyone tried to reach me."

"Jake, you've got to do something quick," Nelle begged.

Helene was looking at her very thoughtfully. "We're going to let the police find you," she said very slowly, "and you're not a blonde. Come out in the bathroom and let me wash your face." She grabbed the black wig from the mantel, shoved Nelle into the bathroom, and shut the door. From behind it Jake could hear water splashing.

"It won't work," Malone said morosely.

"Wait and see," Jake said, sipping his beer.

A few minutes later Helene returned, triumphantly leading the transformed Nelle. The radio singer's golden-brown curls had completely vanished under the bobbed black wig. But that was the smallest part of the change. Nelle Brown had become a very ordinary, pale-faced young woman with dark hair, a small, colorless mouth, and pale eyes behind thick eyeglasses. It seemed to Jake that she had even become smaller and thinner.

"You see?" Helene explained. "The main point is washing off the make-up. It's unbelievable how different a woman looks with her make-up off. Nelle looks like an underfed schoolteacher."

"The important thing is that she doesn't look like Nelle Brown," Jake said. "Besides, the police won't have seen her except in photographs. Her voice would give her away though. Nelle, keep your mouth shut."

"I will."

"You can stay here tonight," he went on. "Tomorrow you can go to rehearsal in that getup. The explanation will be that Nelle Brown is ill and her voice double is rehearsing for her. That's pretty weak, but once you're actually in rehearsal, nobody can get in the studio. It's a chance," he said thoughtfully, "but the one chance."

"Even looking like that," said the young man from next door, "she's wonderful!"

Nelle sat down beside him and began getting acquainted. Helene turned on her radio and then turned it down so low that no one paid any attention to it. Jake and Malone took turns going to the corner for beer. It was nearly eleven o'clock, Helene was discussing with Malone the merits of using gin as a chaser for beer as against using beer as a chaser for gin, when there was a knock on the door. Jake opened it, and ushered in Von Flanagan, accompanied by a weary and morose policeman.

Jake introduced Helene, the black-haired girl (my cousin Miss Wilson, from Lansing, Michigan), and the young man from next door, whose name turned out to be Willie Wolff. Von Flanagan decided he was among friends, sat down, accepted the combination of gin and beer, waved the morose policeman to a chair, and complained bitterly that all people did was conspire to make life hard for him.

"And you, Jake Justus," he concluded, "do you know where this Nelle Brown woman is?"

Jake shook his head. "I wish I did. Have you tried her home?"

"We've been there," Von Flanagan growled. "We've been everywhere. Nobody knows where she is. I'm sick of this damn running around after her. When I do find her, I'm going to throw her in the can."

"On what grounds?" Malone asked.

"She's a material witness," Von Flanagan said. "She came here to see Paul March. This young man here said she did."

"I didn't say it was Nelle Brown," the young man said.

"Well, it sounds like her to me," the police officer growled. "He worked on her radio program, and she's the only blonde we can find who knew him."

"It wasn't Nelle Brown," Helene said suddenly. "It wasn't." To everyone's amazement she suddenly burst into tears.

"What the hell!" Von Flanagan said.

"I didn't want Jake to ever know," Helene said through her sobs, "because we're going to be married, and now you've gone and ruined everything." She wept noisily.

"You mean," Von Flanagan said dazedly, "you mean you were the blonde?" He added absent-mindedly, "Stop crying."

"But I didn't shoot him," Helene sobbed, "I haven't been here for months. Have I, Willie?"

Willie Wolff picked up his cue. "No. No, you haven't."

"You knew it was her all the time and you didn't tell me," Von Flanagan said loudly to the young man. "I oughta arrest you, too."

"I didn't want Mr. Justus to find out," Willie Wolff said hastily.

Helene's weeping became louder.

"Now, now, now," Von Flanagan said soothingly. "Don't cry. Just be calm, and let me ask you a few questions. I said, stop crying. That ain't gonna do you no good. Stop it, I tell you. I've got some questions to ask you. Stop it. God damn it all," he said in a voice that could have been heard halfway across the lake, *"Shut up!"*

Helene gulped, and was obediently silent.

"Now," Von Flanagan said triumphantly, in a tone that conveyed that he knew how to handle these women. "Now you can come along with me, and we'll just have a nice little talk, you and I."

"Look here," Jake said, "you can't do that. She's staying right here."

"Are you telling me what to do?" Von Flanagan asked angrily.

"Jake's right," Malone began. "You can't—"

"You keep out of this," Von Flanagan told him.

"Damn it," Jake said, "I won't have it."

"You shut up," Von Flanagan roared. "That was all I needed, to have you butting in. Come along, sister. We'll see whether I can take you with me or not."

Helene stood up.

"All right," Malone said, "but I'm going with her. I'm her lawyer."

"I'm going, too," Jake said.

"No you aren't," Malone said. "You stay here, Jake."

Jake thought a moment, looked at Miss Wilson from Lansing, and agreed.

"Don't worry," Malone told him, "I'll fix everything up."

Von Flanagan snorted, suddenly also looked at Miss Wilson from Lansing. "You, young lady. Did you ever know Paul March?"

She shook her head.

"What's the matter," the police officer asked, "can't you talk?"

She found a handkerchief, coughed into it, and said in a hoarse and almost indistinguishable voice, "Got a cold."

"Too bad," the policeman said sympathetically, "nasty thing, in this weather. Do you know anything about Paul March?"

"No," said the hoarse voice, "nothing." She coughed again. "I just came down from Lansing for my cousin's wedding."

That seemed to satisfy him. He nodded, said to the morose policeman, "Come along, Konkowski, we got stuff to do," took Helene by the arm, and marched out, Malone following.

The door closed behind them, and heavy footsteps sounded on the stairs. Jake looked accusingly at Miss Wilson from Lansing.

"On top of everything else," he said, "just when I'm about to get married, you go and get my girl thrown into jail."

Her eyes filled with sudden tears. "Oh Jake, I cause you so much trouble. Jake, I'm so sorry. I know I'm nothing but a nuisance."

He patted her shoulder. "Never mind, babe. It's all in the day's work. What have you got a press agent for, anyway? Only we ought to change my contract to Jake Justus and family!"

CHAPTER 31

Jake reminded Nelle that she still had a program to do, induced her to lie down on Helene's bed, and talked to her until she went to sleep. Then he sat by the window and devoted himself to worrying, until sometime near four in the morning when Malone telephoned.

The lawyer informed him that he was letting Von Flanagan keep Helene overnight. It would, he explained, keep his mind off Nelle Brown. Once Jake had delivered Nelle safely to rehearsal, he, Malone, would get Helene out without any difficulty.

Helene was, he added, having a wonderful time.

"She would be," Jake said gloomily, and hung up.

He returned to his chair by the window and sank into a half doze filled with uncomfortable dreams composed of Goldman, the program, Helene, Tootz' horses, and Von Flanagan's mink.

In the morning he sent Nelle to the studio and told her to stay there, met McIvers, observed that the morning papers mentioned only "a blonde woman" being questioned by the police, and went to call on Mr. Goldman.

The sponsor was a small, compact man with white hair and a benevolent face. This morning, however, it was less benevolent than usual, and very anxious.

He showed no indication to waste time discussing fishing, the weather, and what was the matter with the Chicago Cubs. To Jake that was a bad sign.

"It's this way," he said, without preliminaries. "Jake, before I sign the contract tonight, I want that you and Joe should find out who done all these murders."

"I'm afraid I don't understand," Jake said lamely.

"Oh yes, you understand," said Mr. Goldman soothingly. "Oh yes, you do understand, Jake. Suppose I sign the contract tonight, and they don't know yet who done these murders. And maybe tomorrow they find out Nelle, she is mixed up in the murders, or maybe even that she did them herself, only it seems to me like she was too much of a lady. But I'm just supposing, you understand. I ain't saying Nelle is anyway mixed up with these murders, but this man Paul March, he used to be with the show and there was some trouble between him and her when he left it, and this St. John was with the agency, and there was always trouble between him and her. So now I don't want to sign the contract tonight unless I know who done the murders, and that Nelle ain't mixed up in it."

He leaned back, folded his hands across his round little middle, and smiled at them benignly.

"But look here," Jake said, "you can't do this to me. I've arranged for a photographer tonight to take a picture of you and Nelle signing the contract. It's to be announced in the program tonight that the contract is signed for another year. Why, it's written into the script."

"Well," said Mr. Goldman mildly, "I guess maybe you could send the photographer away, and maybe take it out of the script, h'm?"

"Now look, Mr. Goldman," said Joe McIvers, in his most persuasive tone. "You know as well as I do that Nelle Brown couldn't be involved in anything like this. Not Nelle Brown!"

"Maybe so," Mr. Goldman said, "and maybe not so. How should I know? All I say is that I don't sign the contract tonight unless I know who done those murders and that Nelle isn't mixed up in it."

Joe McIvers mopped his forehead.

"Now Mr. Goldman," he said anxiously. "Even if by some wild chance Nelle was involved in this, you could trust Jake to keep it out of the papers. What is he hired for?" He looked hopefully at Jake.

"Sure," Jake said, laughing hollowly. "I could hush it up no matter what happened."

Mr. Goldman pulled his lower lip. "I don't say you can't," he said firmly. "Now look at here. At home I've got a wife and two wonderful daughters. Every week they sit at home and listen to Nelle Brown. Every week they sit at home and tune in the West Coast and hear the rebroadcast of Nelle Brown. Now how would I feel if they sat at home listening to Nelle Brown, and here she is mixed up in two nasty murders."

"But she isn't—" McIvers began.

Mr. Goldman silenced him with a gesture. "All over the country," he said, "people sit at home with their families and listen to Nelle Brown. Now maybe tomorrow they pick up a newspaper and read Nelle Brown is mixed up in a murder mess. Or maybe they don't read about it, but she is just the same. For twenty years," he said oratorically, "for twenty years I have been selling good candy to people. Ever since way back when all I had was a little pushcart and a box of chocolate bars. Then—"

In patient and respectful silence, Jake and Joe McIvers listened to the frequently related story of how Mr. Goldman had risen from his pushcart to become head of the Goldman Candy Company, with products for sale at all candy counters.

"And so," he finished, "Joe, tonight you have my contract there for me to sign, and Jake, you have the photographer there to take the picture, but be sure you have the proof of who murdered those people and that Nelle isn't mixed up in it no way."

"But what can we do?" Joe McIvers asked desperately. "The police are working on the case. What on earth can we do that the police can't do?"

Mr. Goldman shrugged his shoulders. "How should I know? I only make candy. Maybe now Jake here can do something."

"I'm a press agent, not a detective," Jake said, "and there isn't much time before tonight."

"Well," Mr. Goldman said, "you heard what I got to say. That's all." He pushed a button on his desk, and a yellow-haired secretary popped in the door. "Jessie, bring me in those letters I should answer."

"But Mr. Goldman," McIvers began a little desperately.

"Look here," Jake began, "you can't expect—"

Mr. Goldman looked up from the letters on his desk as though surprised to find them still there. "Good-by," he said pleasantly, "I'll see you to-night."

The two men walked silently out.

"Fatheaded old imbecile," McIvers muttered in the elevator. "When he gets set about a thing, you might as well ask the Wrigley Building to waltz as to try to move him."

"No man who can start with a pushcart and make a million bucks in the candy business is a fatheaded old imbecile," Jake observed. "Not as far as I'm concerned, anyway. But this puts us on a nice spot." He sighed. "Maybe it's just that I can't think straight so early in the morning. Let's go talk to Malone."

They found the little lawyer eating breakfast in his office. McIvers told him of Goldman's ultimatum, while Jake helped himself to Malone's coffee.

"What do we do, Malone?" Jake asked.

"Send for more coffee," the lawyer growled. He walked to the window and stood staring gloomily across the rooftops, while Jake sat wondering if Von Flanagan would take him as partner on a mink ranch. By the time Malone's secretary arrived with a thermos bottle of coffee, the lawyer seemed to have reached a decision. He sat down behind his desk and poured coffee into water glasses.

"Helene," Jake asked anxiously, "where's Helene?"

"At the broadcasting studio," Malone said peevishly, "probably telling Nelle Brown how to sing. She put in the night telling Von Flanagan how to run the homicide squad."

Jake sighed with relief. "At least she's out of this mess."

Malone nodded. "It was a matter of proving to Von Flanagan that she really didn't know anything about Paul March," he said, "and she contributed more to that than I did. Then a few hints to Von Flanagan that I might be very displeased, personally, if he didn't forget the whole thing. Don't ask me why that had an effect on him, because I won't tell you. After all, some things are sacred." He sighed heavily. "Anyway, Von Flanagan was damned glad to see the last of her."

In spite of the worries on his mind, Jake grinned at the thought of the havoc Helene must have created at police headquarters. But the grin faded rapidly.

"Malone," he began, wondering if his voice sounded as hoarse as it felt.

"Go on to the rehearsal," the lawyer said wearily. "Act as though nothing at all had happened, and don't let anybody get near Nelle Brown."

"The contract—" Jake said.

"Have it there ready to be signed," Malone told him.

Joe McIvers looked up, the first faint look of hope on his face. "Can you find out who the murderer is in the time we have left?" He paused, gulped, and added, "Do you already know?"

Malone looked at him and said nothing.

"For the love of God, Malone," Jake began.

"Go away," Malone said crossly, "Go away."

"Do you know what you're going to do?"

"I do," Malone said, "and I don't like it. But there's no way out, now. Go away, I want to think."

Jake paused a minute at the door. "Will we see you later?"

"You will," Malone told him. "I'll be at the studio."

"Bringing the murderer with you, I suppose," Jake said sourly.

"He'll be there," Malone growled. "Get the hell out of here."

Jake muttered something about unwashed Irishmen and crooked law-yers, and slammed the door behind him.

"All we can do is hope for the best," he told McIvers. "Malone knows what he's doing. If he says he's going to fix this up, he'll fix it up, so we might as well stop worrying."

"I suppose so," McIvers said. "What shall we do now?"

Jake sighed. "This would be a perfect day to get drunk," he said, "but maybe we'd better get on over to rehearsal."

Schultz was sitting alone in the control room, munching a sandwich and reading *The Daily Racing Form*. He looked up as Jake came in.

"Where'd Nelle get the double?" he asked. "She's a wonder. Sounds almost like Nelle herself."

Jake looked through the window to where Nelle, still wearing the wig, stood by the microphone, arguing about a song arrangement with Lou Silver.

"I don't know where Nelle got her," he said, "but you're right, she's a wonder." He looked around the studio. Yes, there was Helene in a corner, a copy of the script in her lap. The world became a little brighter.

"Of course," Schultz said, brushing a crumb from his chin, "I could tell the difference, being an expert on Nelle's voice, but I'd bet the average listener couldn't. Will she do the show herself? Nelle, I mean?"

"God knows," Jake said, "but I hope so. Look here, Schultz. We're going in there and rehearse. You keep everybody out of here. I don't care who wants to get in the studio or the control room. Keep 'em out—all except a guy named Malone, a lawyer."

"I get you," Schultz said, "I won't let nobody get in."

Jake nodded, walked in the studio, and looked around. There was Helene, looking cool and exquisite in her corner; Nelle, more than ever resem-bling Miss Wilson from Lansing; Lou Silver, marking a last-minute change in an arrangement; Oscar Jepps, coatless, red-faced and perspiring; Bob Bruce, pale and worried; an actress whose name he couldn't remember; two actors whose names he couldn't remember; a bunch of musicians;

Krause fiddling with his sound effects, and Baby. Baby? Oh yes, he remembered. Baby had a part in this week's show.

Oscar saw him and walked across the studio. "What's Nelle wearing the furpiece for?"

"She's a fugitive," Jake said, "don't ask questions. How's the script?"

Oscar said, "I could have written a better one in my sleep."

Nelle joined them. "What goes on?" she asked, very casually.

"Listen," Jake said, "as far as you're concerned, this is just another rehearsal. I want Nelle to keep hidden out for reasons of my own. Schultz is keeping everybody out of the studio, so she might as well take off the disguise. Now get this. The whole mess is going to be cleared up this afternoon. I don't know how myself, but it is. Meanwhile there's a show to do tonight. Forget the whole infernal business and rehearse the show. Now get going."

He signaled to Helene to follow him into the control room, and settled down to listening.

For the first half hour, rehearsal was strained and listless. By the time Jake began to give up hope of an even presentable broadcast, the group began to be too absorbed in the show to think of anything else. By four o'clock, the script had been shortened, lengthened, rearranged, and rewritten, and everyone rested and drank coffee. By five o'clock, a final rehearsal went off with a smoothness and vitality Jake would not have believed possible. As the musicians prepared to leave, he walked into the studio.

"Lou, you can get your boys out of here. You can go, too," he said to the unnamed actress and actors and to Krause. "The rest of you stick around."

"What's up?" Bob Bruce asked.

Jake looked toward the control room and saw Malone. "I think we're going to learn the truth about the murders," he said.

"What murders?" Oscar said innocently, taking his face out of the script.

Jake sighed. "It must be wonderful to be an artist," he remarked, and called into the microphone, "Come on in, Malone."

The little lawyer walked into the studio. He looked very pale and very tired.

"You all know John J. Malone, I guess," Jake said, looking around.

"Have you done something, Malone?" McIvers asked anxiously. "Is the contract safe?"

Malone nodded and sat down heavily in one of the leather-and-chromium chairs. "I know the whole story. I might as well be honest. I've known the important part for several days now." He paused a moment. "There's a way to handle it that will save things, I think. But I hate to do it. Because I know it's going to hurt." He paused again and looked up. "I'm sorry, Nelle. I'm sorrier than I can say."

CHAPTER 32

"What are you talking about?" Jake asked. His voice seemed to come from some perfect stranger.

Malone didn't appear to hear him. He was looking at Nelle. The radio singer seemed to know what he was going to say. She turned very white.

"It isn't worth it," she said. "The contract, the show—nothing is worth it. Nothing in the world."

Malone looked up at her. "It's for you to say," he told her.

"Nelle," McIvers said wildly, "Nelle, the contract."

"Shut up," she said, as casually as though she were slapping a fly. "The program doesn't matter any more. It all seemed so important all along, and now suddenly it isn't." She turned to McIvers. "Joe, you can sell Goldman something else. It'll take a little time, but you can do it. I'm sick of the whole thing anyway. I'm through. I'm not broke. I've saved a hunk of what I've earned this year. Enough for Tootz and me to live on for a while." She flung an arm out in a wide, frantic gesture. "I don't want much. Just Tootz. Just a little corner some-where—where we can settle down and just live and forget all this, and be together, and perhaps find a little happiness someone else hasn't used up. I'm getting out. I'm through with all this. I don't give a damn who murdered Paul March, or Mr. Givvus, or John St. John. I don't give a damn what happens to the program, or the contract, or me. The hell with it all." Her voice broke suddenly.

Oscar Jepps laid a huge paw on her shoulder. "Nelle—"

She didn't seem to know he was there.

"I'm sorry, Nelle," Malone said again. "I'm sorry. It was the only way. And it's too late to stop things now."

He looked toward the door. All their eyes followed his. The door opened slowly, very slowly, and Henry Gibson Gifford, very digni-fied, very beautifully dressed, and very debonair, walked into the stu-dio.

"I'm glad I heard your speech, Nelle," he said quietly, "even though you didn't mean it for me." He laid his hat and stick on a chair, very deliberately.

"You heard it!" Nelle said.

"Through the loud-speaker," he explained, "in the control room. The operator had you still—hooked up is the word, isn't it?"

"But how did you get here?" Nelle asked. "You didn't come here alone! You couldn't have—"

"I telephoned him," Malone said wearily. "I telephoned and said Nelle was in danger of arrest. I thought he'd come here. I had to find out, some-way, if he'd go out alone, without Nelle. I mean—I had to prove it. I knew."

"Oh no," Nelle said, "no. It can't be this way."

"It was the only thing I could do for you," Henry Gibson Gifford said very simply. He reached in his pocket, took out a little package, and gave it to her. "This is the only thing I have ever been able to give you. I meant to send it, anonymously. Perhaps this was the better way after all."

She took the package almost mechanically, released the rubber band that held it, saw that it contained letters.

"But where," she began, and stopped. "Where did you get these?"

"From John St. John's pocket," Malone answered.

Jake's hand groped for a chair. "You mean," he said, "you mean that *he*—" He paused and frowned. "But Malone, you said yourself that he wasn't—mad. Not that kind of madness."

"These murders were committed by a sane man," Malone said. "That was the key to the whole thing, that he was sane."

His eyes and the fine gray eyes of Henry Gibson Gifford met in a look of understanding that excluded everyone else in the room.

"When did you know?" the white-haired man said.

"It was Jake who told me first," Malone said. "It was Jake who made me see the whole thing." He turned to Jake. "First, when you said—'It's a good thing Tootz isn't sane, or this situation would drive him crazy!' "

Jake nodded slowly.

"That told me," Malone said, "and then there was another thing, more definite. Tootz would not go out of the apartment without Nelle. That was pointed out to me time and again. Yet on two separate times when Jake telephoned the apartment, no one answered the telephone. Tootz would have answered if he had been there. And both times, we knew that he was not with Nelle. Obviously, he must have gone out alone. If he would do that—he was sane."

"I don't understand at all," Nelle said.

Malone smiled at her very gently. "When you married him, he was a very wealthy man. He adored you. He looked forward to giving you everything you wanted. Then suddenly he lost everything.

"You came home and told him you'd signed the contract for your program. He was just realizing that he was through, finished. Suddenly the whole situation was reversed. From then on you'd be supporting not only yourself but him, and the whole world would know. That afternoon—was the first time Henry Gibson Gifford thought he saw horses in the living room."

There was a long silence.

"You mean," Nelle said, "he pretended?" Suddenly she flung herself on her knees in front of Tootz' chair, grasped his hands. "You pretended, all the time? You never saw any horses? Not any at all?"

"Not any horses at all," he said softly, "nor any men following me." He looked over her head and smiled at Malone. "You must admit the horses were a very nice touch, though."

"They were," Malone said. "A very nice touch."

"But why?" Nelle demanded wildly. "Why?"

He stroked her soft, shining hair very tenderly. "Perhaps I should simply have gone away. Perhaps I should have gone out a window, as so many men did. But you were too precious to me, Nelle. Precious, and I felt too that you needed me. Yet—I couldn't simply stay on and be the bankrupt husband of Nelle Brown, living on the income from her artistry. I could stay and be a harmless old madman. Do you understand? Do you forgive me, Nelle?"

"You talk of forgiveness," Malone said, "after what you have done for her?"

"The imaginary men following me," the old man went on, continuing to stroke her hair, "were for another reason. I wanted to know all that was going on. I knew you were as impulsive as a child. I thought there might be a time when you would need help, protection perhaps. When everyone believed I wouldn't leave the house without Nelle, I always had a perfect alibi whenever Nelle was away."

Jake looked up. "That's what's been fooling me all along," he said.

The white-haired man nodded. "I didn't plan it as an alibi for murder. But it came in very handily. I planned it so that I could keep an eye on Nelle." The graceful old fingers paused, half tangled in her hair. "I knew all about Paul March. It all but broke my heart that I couldn't comfort you when you needed it so. I knew all about"—he looked up to smile at Baby—"this young man. Those things haven't mattered. Only your goodness to me mattered."

Nelle was very still, her face buried on his knee.

"I knew what Paul March was, and I was afraid for you. Then that night a week ago you brought your script home, and I glanced through it and saw the impression left by his note to you. I knew, then, that the only thing to do was to kill him."

Jake had never known that a room could be so still.

"I remembered the program that came just after yours, and I was sure the sound of the shots in that program would cover the sound of mine. I was confident Paul March would have his radio on, turned to your program, and I was right. I was in the hall just as your program finished, listened for the start of the other one, and walked in without knocking. He was in the kitchenette. I went up to him and shot him."

There was a long silence. Jake felt Helene's hand, very cold, slip into his own.

Henry Gibson Gifford drew a long, sighing breath. "The letters were in his pocket. I looked for any other reminder of you, Nelle, and found nothing. But I found money in his wallet, and that bothered me. I knew you hadn't come and bought the letters. Finally I concluded he must have been blackmailing someone else.

"Just then I heard your steps in the hall. I hid out on the fire escape and watched you search the room."

She looked up suddenly. "Then I was being watched when I was in that room! I felt it—and yet I thought it wasn't possible." She caught her breath sharply. "I was watched—and by you!" She buried her face again.

The old man went on as though there had been no interruption. "There was now another danger. Your coming to the apartment might involve you when the murder was discovered. Then this young man"—he indicated Baby—"came, and I stayed on the fire escape until he had gone. Then I stayed there trying to think what to do, and while I was there, first Jake arrived, and then McIvers. I stayed out on the fire escape nearly two hours while a perfect procession of people came into that room." He paused and smiled. "It was almost like watching a parade."

Jake cleared his throat harshly. "All that was needed was a guide and a rubberneck wagon."

Tootz' gray eyes met his appreciatively.

"Then I," Joe McIvers began, and stopped to stare at the old man. "You must have thought I was insane."

Henry Gibson Gifford shook his head. "I understand why you were doing what you did. But when you moved the body of Paul March, I followed you and saw you hide it in the old warehouse."

Joe McIvers blinked. "I didn't dream that anyone was watching me— following me."

Tootz smiled. "I was very quiet." He paused and drew a long, sighing breath. "I thought everything was settled. Sooner or later the body of Paul March would need to be destroyed. There was no immediate hurry. I knew that when the time came, a fire in the old warehouse would cause an explosion in the refrigerating chamber that would probably destroy the body beyond recognition." He smiled wryly. "When that time came, I didn't know that the body had been removed.

"I'm afraid," he said slowly, "I'm afraid I bungled things badly."

In the long silence that followed, his fingers began stroking Nelle's hair again, slowly and rhythmically.

"But damn it all," Helene began. Her voice broke off suddenly, she scowled and began again, "You said you took the letters from Paul March's pocket. Then how did St. John get hold of them? What happened to St. John?" She paused and scowled again. "And Mr. Givvus. None of this explains who murdered Mr. Givvus."

Henry Gibson Gifford nodded toward the letters Nelle still held limply in her hands.

"They explain who killed Mr. Givvus," he said quietly. "Who and why. They explain—everything you asked."

CHAPTER 33

Nelle picked up the big envelope and shook it. Three packages of letters fell onto the studio floor. Jake picked them up, stared at them.

"But they're all alike," he exclaimed.

Malone almost grabbed them from his hand.

Henry Gibson Gifford said, "Paul March was a forger as well as a blackmailer."

Malone was looking hard at the letters. "There were three sets of letters, exactly the same!" He looked up at the old man.

"Paul March was a clever man," Gifford said. "He knew of three people who would be customers for them, so he forged two duplicate sets of letters. I don't know myself which is the real set. Yes, a clever lad. Too bad he ended up as he did—he could have gone far in the world." He reached in the big envelope, pulled out several notes written on odds and ends of paper and handed them to Malone. "Those are even more explanatory."

Malone took them, handed the three sets of letters to Nelle. She looked at them a little stupidly.

"But where were these others?" she asked. "Who had them?"

"St. John had one set, bought from Paul March," Henry Gibson Gifford said. "Mr. Givvus of Philadelphia had the other, also bought from Paul March."

"He had them," Malone said, looking up, "until St. John killed him for them."

After the very long pause that followed, Joe McIvers said, "You can't tell me an agency man would shoot his own prospective client." He took a long breath and added, "Especially before an audition."

Malone, musing, ignored him. "That explains why Givvus had sent Paul March five hundred dollars. As near as I can tell from this correspondence between Givvus and St. John—heaven knows why St. John didn't destroy it when he had the chance—Paul March evidently knew what the situation was regarding the Nelle Brown Revue—as far as St. John's hopes of selling it to Givvus was concerned. Evidently he also knew Givvus, and what Givvus would try to do if he had the chance. At any rate, he sold a set of the letters to Givvus."

Tootz nodded. "That's how I figured it out myself."

"Then," Malone went on thoughtfully, "when Givvus turned up for the audition, he told St. John that he had his own hold over Nelle Brown and was going to get her show on his own terms, by dealing direct with her, leaving St. John out of the picture. It would have saved Givvus a pile of money. St. John not only saw his own plans go haywire, but he knew that unless he could get Givvus out of the way, he couldn't sell Nelle Brown to anyone else. With Givvus dead, he could. St. John needed the money and prestige desperately."

The lawyer scowled. "Naturally everyone assumed that the last person in the world who would have shot Givvus was St. John. As Joe here just said— no agency man would shoot his own client, especially after arranging an audition for him. We all jumped to that conclusion, and St. John knew we would. That audition was arranged to conceal a murder. It must have happened that way. St. John ushered him into the client's room as soon as he arrived, killed him before the audition, and took the duplicates of Nelle's letters and his own notes to Givvus out of the dead man's pockets."

"But St. John—" Joe McIvers began a little stupidly.

The old man interrupted him. "I thought everything was all right—that every danger was out of the way. Then St. John came to see Nelle, and told her *he* had the letters. She thought I was taking a nap at the time he was there—I wasn't. I was listening. I knew I had the letters taken from Paul March's pockets. Finally, I came to a conclusion which proved to be the right one—that there were duplicate letters.

"At first, I wasn't sure what to do. I knew Nelle didn't want to give the audition, and I knew the reason why she was doing it. Then when Mr. Givvus of Philadelphia turned up on a bench in Lincoln Park, I didn't know what had happened. I did know, though, that St. John was a danger to Nelle. The letters he had might be duplicates—but they were just as great a threat to her as those I had taken from Paul March's pockets. So I knew St. John had to die."

Once more the slim old fingers paused, half tangled in Nelle's hair.

"I went to St. John's house. He was asleep before his radio. No one else was there. I turned the loud-speaker on full to cover the sound of the shot, and killed him. The letters were in his pocket. I took them, and then I knew that Nelle was safe."

In the long silence that followed, Nelle looked up at Malone. "How did you know? How did you find it out?"

"I didn't know," the little lawyer said, "I didn't know. I had to guess." His voice was very tired. "But everything that happened was to your benefit. That, in my mind, narrowed it down to those who loved you enough to commit murder for you.

"But it could be Tootz," he went on, "only if he were sane. That was the balance point on which the whole thing rested. If his delusions were real"— he smiled—"well, leave it that way. If his delusions were real, it was true that he wouldn't leave the apartment without you, and in that case, he couldn't possibly have committed the murders. But if he were sane, his delusion of the men following him and his refusal to leave the apartment gave him a perfect alibi. Because of that chance remark of Jake's—and because the evidence of the telephone calls indicated that he had been out of the apartment without Nelle on two separate occasions—I believed that he was sane.

"Up to the very last," he said softly, "up to the very minute when he appeared in the shadows of the control room, listening to what Nelle was saying, I wasn't sure. It was a shot in the dark, though I was fairly sure of my aim. When I telephoned him that Nelle was in danger of arrest, I knew that if he were sane, he would come here. If he were not, then my whole theory was wrong, and the game was up, as far as the program and Nelle's contract were concerned."

"Damn you," Jake said in a sudden rage, "damn you, Malone. All this hasn't done any good. It's found the murderer, yes—but you've made everything worse than ever. Goldman will never sign the contract after hearing this. Tootz will go to jail for the rest of his life, and that's all the good you've done."

"No," Malone said thoughtfully, "Tootz won't go to jail. Because outside of the people in this room, no one knows that he isn't mad."

A smile crossed the handsome face of Henry Gibson Gifford. "I haven't a very long time to live," he said. "I'd hate to spend it in a penitentiary. But they don't send madmen there, do they, Malone?"

"No," Malone said, "a pleasanter place. And Nelle will have nothing but the sympathy of the world when the news breaks that her half-mad husband had gone completely mad, homicidal. Even Goldman will sympathize with that. You, Jake, should be able to see that."

The old man said, "A quiet room in a pleasant place, with a radio set perhaps, and Nelle to visit me now and then—I couldn't ask for much more."

Malone stood up. "Shall we go, Gifford? If those horses could convince people all these months, they'll convince Von Flanagan now."

Nelle rose, clasped Tootz' hand. Jake tried not to look at her face.

"You mustn't cry," Henry Gibson Gifford said very gently. "You'll hurt your throat. And you have a program to do tonight."

"Yes," she said, "I have a program to do tonight, and a week from to-night and a week from then—" Her voice broke ever so little. "If you could do this for me, Tootz, I guess I can live up to it."

He kissed her once, said, "I'm ready to go, Malone," and walked to the studio door without looking back, as though he had been on his way to receive a decoration.

Nelle stood very still, looking after him. No one spoke. Jake counted the squares in the studio floor and wished someone would say something, felt that someone, anyone, must speak, must say something, anything. And at last it was his own voice that he heard.

"Nelle, you can't do the program in that dress."

The tension broke, everyone seemed ready to speak at once.

Nelle seemed to wake from a dream, looked at her watch. "But I'd have to go home to change. And there isn't time before the broadcast."

Then Helene came to life again. "Oh yes there is," she said, "oh yes there is. Have you ever seen me drive?"

CHAPTER 34

In Von Flanagan's dingy little office, Henry Gibson Gifford, otherwise Tootz, had finished telling his story of how he had eluded the watchful eye of Nelle Brown and shot and killed Paul March, Mr. Givvus, and John St. John, because they were persecuting him. Something told him to do it, he explained. He produced the gun that had shot March and St. John, apologized for having lost the gun that shot Mr. Givvus, and gave the one he had to Von Flanagan with a little sigh of regret.

The only thing he didn't confess to, Malone said later, was Helene's driving through a red light.

"We should of known it," Von Flanagan said to Malone. "We knew Nelle Brown had a husband who was a little over the sill, but we never thought he'd go completely off. We should of seen that these murders were committed by a nut—anybody with half an eye should of seen it right away."

Malone smiled modestly.

"This sure is tough for her," Von Flanagan said sympathetically. "We'll make it as easy as we can for her. Not much fuss, a simple commitment. Everybody knows he's been crazy for months. Yes, we'll make it as easy as we can for her. Did you get me her autograph?"

"I will," Malone promised.

Von Flanagan turned to Henry Gibson Gifford. "How'd you come to pick those particular guys?"

Henry Gibson Gifford leaned forward confidentially. "I thought I had to shoot everybody who had anything to do with the radio program. Everybody. I had to. Only Mr. Malone convinced me I ought to tell you about it first."

Von Flanagan nodded sympathetically.

"It beats all how a frail little guy could of moved those bodies," he said reflectively.

"Bigges never knew I had the car," the old man said boastfully, "and I'm strong. I wanted to hide them all in the old warehouse, but I was afraid. It made a nice fire, the whole warehouse. I wish I could see another fire." He sighed regretfully. "Mr. Malone says I've got to go away somewhere. But I don't mind. It's all right as long as I can take the horses with me."

Von Flanagan looked up, puzzled. "Horses?"

Henry Gibson Gifford looked all around the room, and smiled. "Horses. My horses." He said it so convincingly that for a moment the police officer caught himself looking around to see if they were really there. Then his eyes met Malone's in a long glance of deep and sympathetic understanding.

There were only those last few minutes before the show went on the air. Jake Justus stretched his long legs in the control room and wished the next half hour was safely over.

Papa Goldman had been extremely sympathetic. The occurrence would make Nelle Brown a heroine in the eyes of her public. Malone had promised that the story would not break until after the rebroadcast for the Coast. In the meantime there would be the show; after the show the contract would be signed. Right now the photographer was waiting in the studio lobby.

Everything was settled, everything was serene. Nelle was out of trouble. The contract would be re-signed. In—he looked up at the control-room clock—thirty-three minutes and fifteen seconds the show would be over.

That is, if Helene had managed to get Nelle back to the studio in time! For a horrible moment he thought of everything that might happen—accidents, arrests, traffic jams.

In the studio Bob Bruce, serene and smiling, was making his regular weekly spiel about the show, the star, and the sponsor, and "Quiet in the studio, please, except when laughter or applause are indicated." Bob Bruce was pale, but his face was happy. He was going to see Essie St. John after the rebroadcast.

Joe McIvers tiptoed into the studio, his long, thin face pleasant and relieved.

Everyone was happy, Jake thought, except Nelle. Nelle was the one who had been hurt. How would she ever go through a broadcast after what had happened in the afternoon? But she would. She'd make it the show of a lifetime, so that listeners all over the nation, picking up their newspapers tomorrow morning, would remember it. After the broadcast, what?

There was Baby, standing among the members of the dramatic cast, anxiously watching the studio door. What was it Baby had said? Oh yes. "When it does come, if somebody like me is there—" Well, he was there.

Someday Nelle Brown would abandon him as casually and carelessly as she would abandon a song she had sung too many times, but this was Baby's hour.

Even in the glass booth, he was aware of the sudden hush, the breathless expectancy that had come over the studio audience.

"—and here she is herself, ladies and gentlemen, the star of Nelle Brown's Revue—Nelle Brown in person!" (*Applause cue.*)

There she was, and Jake sighed with relief. She was back in time.

The control-room door closed behind him, and Helene slipped into the chair by his side.

"Special permission to sit in the control room," Schultz said with a grin, offering Helene a chocolate.

How pale Nelle was!

The sign-off of the program just ending came suddenly from the control-room loud-speaker. Jake held his breath.

There was the station break, and the chimes. Then Schultz made a sudden, rapid twisting of dials, a quick, emphatic signal to the studio, whispered, "Take the baby," as though they could hear him through the pane of glasss, and drew a bag of salted peanuts from his pocket to eat during the show.

And then her voice filled the little, silent room—warm, rich, dramatic, and calm as a lake at early evening.

"Golden moon—over the midnight sky—"

Jake suddenly remembered one line he had intended to suggest revising.

Well, there was no revising to be done now.

He settled back in his uncomfortable chromium-and-leather chair, and laid his hand over Helene's.

Twenty-nine minutes and forty seconds later he reflected that it had been the best show of the series. Everything was settled, everything was perfect. It was just a great big wonderful world.

All except one thing.

He sat straight up in his chair and swore unhappily.

There wasn't time to drive to Crown Point and be married between broadcasts!

THE END

About the Rue Morgue Press

"Rue Morgue Press is the old-mystery lover's best friend, reprinting high quality books from the 1930s and '40s."
—*Ellery Queen's Mystery Magazine*

Since 1997, the Rue Morgue Press has reprinted scores of traditional mysteries, the kind of books that were the hallmark of the Golden Age of detective fiction. Authors reprinted or to be reprinted by the Rue Morgue include Catherine Aird, Delano Ames, H. C. Bailey, Morris Bishop, Nicholas Blake, Dorothy Bowers, Pamela Branch, Joanna Cannan, John Dickson Carr, Glyn Carr, Torrey Chanslor, Clyde B. Clason, Joan Coggin, Manning Coles, Lucy Cores, Frances Crane, Norbert Davis, Elizabeth Dean, Carter Dickson, Eilis Dillon, Michael Gilbert, Constance & Gwenyth Little, Marlys Millhiser, Gladys Mitchell, Patricia Moyes, James Norman, Stuart Palmer, Craig Rice, Kelley Roos, Charlotte Murray Russell, Maureen Sarsfield, Margaret Scherf, Juanita Sheridan and Colin Watson..

To suggest titles or to receive a catalog of Rue Morgue Press books write 87 Lone Tree Lane, Lyons, CO 80540, telephone 800-699-6214, or check out our website, www.ruemorguepress.com, which lists complete descriptions of all of our titles, along with lengthy biographies of our writers.